SAVED BY FAITH

JENNA BRANDT

COPYRIGHT

This book was previously published under the title, Love's Mending Embrace while it was a part of Melissa Storm's First Street Church Kindle World as well as Promised to a Soldier in The Rockwood Springs Series. Both versions were set in WWI but the book has been edited to remove references to that world and era and has been updated with new content, characters and historical information to reflect the civil war era. Names and places have been changed for historical accuracy.

-To Dustin-
You're my personal soldier.
Thank you for fighting for us.

CHAPTER 1

Late August 1864
Myrtle Grove, South Carolina

Faith Abernathy looked up into the afternoon sky as sweat trickled down the back of her neck and face. Clouds formed in the distance, which meant the imminence of rain. Rich soil overwhelmed her nose while her heart ached at the thought of not finishing the yam harvest before the storm arrived. Though it was dismal, it would be all they had to eat for the foreseeable future.

Three years ago, she never would have thought she would be forced to trade her life of elegant dinners and fancy balls for one filled with back-breaking labor. Starvation was a harsh master, bringing everyone to their knees. She was only grateful her family hadn't been forced to steal to survive, at least not yet. The war wasn't over, and there was no definitive end in sight.

The Confederacy insisted that in the end they were going to win, but with the recent heavy losses they had sustained, Faith wondered if the entire war was for naught. Already things were different and would never be the same again. Most plantations were in ruins either from untended crops or burnt out husks from Union soldiers. Wealthy southern families, like her own, that had thrived for generations, were reduced to poverty, and the very institution of slavery the Confederacy had fought to preserve was all but gone now. Though her own family had only used free workers, she knew that many other plantations depended on the system to sustain their way of life. Many of the Southern slaves, once seemingly loyal, had run away and joined the Union forces, adding even more turmoil to dire circumstances. With everything destroyed around them, she wondered how desperate her fellow Southerners would get before the war ended.

She raised her hand and placed it over her brow. Her brothers were playing instead of working at the other end of the field. With a shout, Faith warned, "Boys, get back to your task."

Her brother, Davis, shrugged. "I don't need your bossing. You're only older by a year," he teased in a Southern accent, common with most of the townspeople.

They must have gotten the point though because after a few moments, both her brothers returned to picking.

Faith wiped the sweat from her forehead with the edge of the apron she wore over her dirty dress, then re-adjusted the scarf which covered her long blonde hair, equally soiled from the long hours of work.

As she placed the produce into the wooden pail, she sang a hymn she had learned Sunday. Church was a reprieve, a solitary hour in which her thoughts weren't fixated on the war and her fiancé, Nathan Maddox.

She remembered the final moments they had spent together before he reported for duty with the military. When Faith closed her eyes, she could still sense the warmth of his arms around her as she basked in his loving embrace.

"It won't be permanent. Keep faith in God and us because I'm coming home to you," he vowed.

As she rested her head against his chest, she argued, "It's not fair. You served your time. Why do they need you again?"

"I must do my part for our safety. Promise me, you'll wait until I return."

Faith did not waiver. "Always and forever."

Nathan leaned towards her and placed his lips on hers. It was a searing kiss, and it branded Faith his for eternity.

Over a half a year had passed since his departure. In the beginning, he wrote often, but the war continued to claim larger chunks of his time. As of late, the letters were sporadic in arrival, prompting Faith to worry without end.

Daily, she feared receiving the news of Nathan's death, and as each week dragged by without communication, the concern deepened. During the day, she kept busy helping with the chores around the plantation, focusing on everything besides missing Nathan. At night with no distractions, however, the longing for him overwhelmed her. She missed staring into his bright blue eyes and running her fingers through his thick, dark hair.

Faith knew she needed to trust God to protect the man she loved, so she whispered a quick, familiar prayer as she placed more yams into the bucket.

A tear slipped down Faith's cheek, which she

quickly swiped away. "There's no time for tears," Faith chastised herself. "I need to get these vegetables picked before the clouds come overhead."

Most Southerners faced financial burdens due to the war, and every penny was precious. The family's survival depended on the crops. Due to most of their workers running off or taking up with the Confederate military, the family had been left to try to sustain the plantation alone.

"What are you doing?"

Faith swiveled around to find her eight-year-old sister, Nancy, standing behind her. With a smile, she brushed the brown curls from her sibling's face. "Picking yams."

Her sister looked in the pail with skepticism. "You haven't finished much since Ida returned home."

As Faith glanced into her bucket, the emptiness shocked her. She should've noticed her slowed pace since their sister, Ida, had left. Chagrined, Faith tried to deflect, "What gives you that idea?"

"Because Ida brought two pails back over an hour ago."

For being so young, Nancy was astute. Faith blushed, feeling as though the red poured out from her green eyes to her muddy, boot-covered toes. It was vital that she finish her job before dusk. With a sigh, she turned to pick the vegetables again.

"I could help if you want. Mother told me I didn't have to be back until supper since it's Ida's turn to work in the kitchen."

Faith stopped and spun around, raising one eyebrow. "And why volunteer to aid me when you could play?"

"Because that's what sisters do; they help each other."

Embarrassed over her suspicion, tears came to the corner of Faith's eyes again. "Thank you, Nancy. I appreciate your offer." She reached out and handed a pail to her sibling.

Faith sang, with her sister joining in, as they gathered up the remaining yams. Her spirits were lifted by her sister's presence and her longing for Nathan ebbed for the time being.

CHAPTER 2

Early September 1864
Undisclosed location, Union Territory

The cold sweat from the preceding hours still clung to Nathan Maddox's broken body as every inch ached with immeasurable pain. His wrists cried out for release from the ropes binding his arms behind the rickety, wooden chair he had sat in for countless days.

Nathan closed his swollen eyes and pictured better times before the talk of war had tainted everything. He remembered standing in the fields fresh after harvest, listening to Pastor Howell speak Sunday mornings at church, and his fiancée, Faith's, welcoming smile. If he kept his mind focused on his life in Myrtle Grove, he could survive this.

Nathan let his mind drift back to his favorite memory.

It was a warm summer evening as Faith curled up in the corner of his arm. They had stolen away from the elaborate party still in full swing in the nearby massive ballroom of the Abernathy plantation.

The stars were shining bright and the night was flawless as they danced on the long, wraparound veranda that encompassed the back part of the house. It overlooked the gardens, which were glistening under the moonlight.

"The sky is so brilliant tonight. I can see every star," Faith whispered in his ear as he held her close.

"It's beautiful, though not as magnificent as you look tonight in that gown."

Faith looked perfect in her golden gown made of satin. It shimmered under the starlight and swished as it moved along the ground. Her white, full-length, silk gloves were smooth under his touch, but not as smooth as her skin, which he could feel where his own hand touched her back.

"I can't wait until we're married and don't have to sneak away like this," Faith sighed. *"I can't wait to be your wife."*

"I'm only grateful your father is allowing me to marry you. I know I don't come from a family like yours, but I will do right by you, Faith, I promise."

"I know you will, Nathan. My father does too, and that's why he agreed to let you marry me. You worked hard, earning your right to be the foreman of my family's plantation. You've proven to everyone what a good and honorable man you are."

"I know some still think it wrong he relented to our union, but I—"

"Shh," Faith whispered, placing her gloved finger against his lips. "You need not explain yourself to me or anyone else. I only wish that we could be married this very night, that this ball was to celebrate our wedding, and not another charity event for the war."

"I know, and as soon as I finish building the house on the land I bought from your father, we can wed," Nathan stated with a smile. "It will be nice to settle into our own life together once it's done."

"How long before you think they'll finish?" Faith inquired with a hint of impatience in her voice.

"Only a few more months. Then we can get married and start our family." Nathan pulled back to stare into Faith's eyes. "The night is perfect, but nothing compares to you."

Faith smiled as she placed her gloved hand on the side of his face. "I love you so much, Nathan. I look forward to being your wife and making you happy for the rest of our lives."

"You've got it backward. It's my job to make you happy and I plan to be an expert at it."

With a laugh, she stated, "You're already off to a terrific start."

Nathan pressed his lips against Faith's in another tender kiss. He savored holding her in his arms and the warmth of her lips against his own.

"I love you, Faith, always and forever."

Laughter outside his room jerked Nathan back to the present. He wished he could have stayed in the memory of Faith forever; however, he was forced to return to the awful place he was being held in.

He sent up a prayer, knowing that only through God's strength could he bear what was coming. As long as he remembered what he was living for, he could survive what was to come. "Please Lord, give me the courage I need to endure this trial, for I'm nothing without you. Help me to not surrender to what they want from me. Comfort Faith as I'm separated from her. I know you'll protect us both."

His biggest regret was his decision to fake his age and enlist in the military as a young boy of sixteen. Nathan had done it for the wrong reason; the product of a childhood spent in orphanages with scarce food to eat and ragged clothes. A seasoned officer saw his desperation and preyed on it. He recognized desperate men will do desperate acts. Nathan willingly signed his life away just for his basic needs to be met.

"Join us, and you'll never be without again," the officer had promised him. He didn't tell him what Nathan would lose in return.

Trained to be a spy's spy after he had first joined the military, Nathan's unassuming looks worked well for him. Even now at 23, he looked years younger. Coupled with his shrewd intellect and ability to adapt to any situation, Nathan fit perfectly as an infiltrator.

A shiver surged through him as he thought how devoid of emotions he used to be. He had learned to push away any real sense of compassion, as it had no place in the job he did. However, over time, his assignments had taken their toll.

If only he had known the Lord before he had entered the military, but he hadn't found salvation until three years after in a rural Northern town. The details were etched in Nathan's memory.

Nathan tried to dismiss the disgust he felt for himself over what he had done the previous day. He had located a lead on a traitor by lying to an unsuspecting source for several weeks. Nathan had been effective in his deception, pretending to care about the traitor's niece to gain her trust. As quickly as he got the information, he disappeared, leaving the woman without so much as a goodbye.

The snow flurries were drifting as Nathan opened the door. He felt the flakes land on his face and melt, leaving a wet kiss upon his cheeks. A chill shot down his spine and he pulled his coat around him tighter. As he placed his foot upon the slick ground outside, he lost his footing and found himself falling. He hit the earth with a thud and the wind was knocked from him.

"Are you all right?"

Nathan looked up to find a stranger offering a helping hand. As he looked into the other man's kind, brown eyes, he was compelled to learn what made the stranger so caring.

After the man with dark-hair and friendly smile helped him up, he offered to treat Nathan to a cup of coffee around the corner at a café. He wasn't sure why he accepted the invitation, but he found himself sitting in a wooden chair across from the man, who was much older than himself.

Nathan watched as he politely conversed with the server, who in turn, smiled and laughed at the man's jokes. He had a calming ease Nathan had never witnessed before, which instantly drew people to him.

"Why are you the way you are?" Nathan blurted out. Normally, he would wait, get to know his target and coax out the information he wanted, but this man had a way of making him act contrary to his normal self.

"Shouldn't we introduce ourselves first? I'm Peter Hawarden and I'm a pastor here in Greenville."

Nathan flinched and looked away. He was religious. Nathan had never found comfort in organized religion. At the orphanage, they tried to force it on him, but he had resisted. He had wanted nothing to do with a belief system that allowed nuns to treat orphans the way they did at that horrible place.

"Are you going to tell me your name?"

He should lie to him considering why he was in town, but before he could stop it, "Nathan Maddox," slipped from his mouth.

Why did he just do that? This man seemed to cause him to go against all his training.

"Well, Nathan, to answer your earlier question, I believe in God and He makes me the way I am." Peter stared at Nathan for several seconds before he asked, "The real question is why do you want to know?"

It was a good question. Now that Nathan had the answer, did he plan to do anything about it? Peter didn't act like the few Christians he had met over the years, which meant not all Christians were the same. Was it possible that depending on a person's relationship with God, you were a different person? If that were the case, maybe religion wasn't *bad at its roots, but simply depended on the person wielding it.*

"I asked because I want what you have. You seem to have a peace I want to feel."

"Then all you have to do is accept Jesus as your Savior. I can show you how."

Nathan nodded as the man asked him to bow his head and repeat after him. Nathan felt relief flood him as he repeated the words.

Once Nathan became a Christian, there was no turning back. When he had returned for reassignment, he had turned in his letter of separation. He was a new man, and wanted to leave the world of lies and secrets behind him.

The solitary door to the room opened and slammed shut, breaking his train of thought. Footsteps echoed as they approached, and Nathan steeled himself for what was next. The Union officers would continue their task of breaking him.

"Have you reconsidered your position, Nathan, and come to the right conclusion?"

Nathan stared at his persecutor, Christopher Berns, without blinking. "My duty has not changed, and so, I must stay unyielding in my decision. Do what you wish with me, but I'll never give you the information you want."

Christopher growled under his breath, his Southern accent emerging for a moment. "The means of persuasion we've been using over the last few weeks have been unsuccessful. I expected as much considering your past training. I suppose it's time to move on to more compelling methods."

Nathan wore the marks of the earlier techniques across his body. Lacerations, bruises, and burns blanketed his physique. His left leg tilted at an odd angle and his ribs hurt with every breath. His refusal to comply had increased the amount and cruelty of his torture. The instant he saw Christopher standing before him, he knew the severity would be immense; Nathan had trained him well.

The U.S. government had assumed it was a victory when Nathan recruited the son of a large plantation owner who agreed to spy for them. Christopher socialized in circles that made him the perfect candidate to train for espionage. But what Nathan didn't know because he had already left the military by the time the war started, was that Christopher had been tasked to spy for the Union on the Confederacy. When his true allegiance was discovered, Christopher fled to the North, taking his training and knowledge with him.

When the Confederate government realized

Nathan's connection to Christopher, they conscripted him and assigned him to track Christopher down and neutralize him. When Nathan had arrived in Boston, it didn't go unnoticed, resulting in Christopher setting an ambush for Nathan. The student had out-maneuvered the teacher.

"You can do your worst, but my God will sustain me," Nathan stated with firm resolve. He didn't want Christopher knowing that he was already beginning to wear down from the immense torture he'd sustained. He wasn't sure how much more he could take.

"We shall see if you still believe in God after I finish with you."

The crack of the whip filled the room, but by God's boundless mercy, Nathan only heard the sound of Faith's loving voice.

CHAPTER 3

The townspeople watched as Faith walked into the church. She sensed the sympathetic looks on their faces and felt her body blush with discomfort. The entire population of Myrtle Grove was aware Nathan had been reported missing and presumed dead.

Bonnie Baker, the town gossip, sprang up from her seat and made her way over to Faith. She reached out and took Faith's hand in her own. Bonnie's Southern accent was thick and she trilled her r's. "Dear, I'm so sorry to hear what happened to your poor Nathan. Whatever are you gonna do?"

Stiffening from resolve, Faith stated with conviction, "Nathan isn't dead. He's far too capable to die in the war. The confederacy has misinformed us."

Faith wasn't sure whom she was trying to convince more, Bonnie or herself. Maybe if she spoke her hopes out loud enough, her heart would stop beating with fear that the news was based on truth.

"Oh, dear, you're still in shock." Bonnie gave Faith a pitying look. "It'll get better. You have everyone in Myrtle Grove to help you through this. You don't have to go through it alone."

Several more people approached Faith, giving their condolences over her loss. With each person, she wanted to scream at the top of her lungs that it wasn't true. It couldn't be because she would know it in her heart. She wasn't sure what happened to him, but she knew Nathan wasn't dead.

By the time service was about to begin, Faith felt like she was a volcano on the verge of erupting. The pity everyone poured out on her was the worst. She knew they thought she was deluding herself. She resisted the urge to snap and forced another smile instead. "Thank you, Mr. and Mrs. Stine, I appreciate your support along with everyone else's."

Her mother must have noticed Faith's distress. As she approached the group of people surrounding her daughter, gratitude filled Faith's heart. "It's time we sit, Faith. It looks as if Pastor Howell is getting ready to start."

Pastor George Howell was the grandson of the founder of Myrtle Grove Church and was a third-generation pastor. From his managing of church member problems to his ability to speak into the hearts of the congregation, it was obvious he had grown up in a family of church leaders.

As the Abernathys made their way to their usual pew at the front of the church, Faith leaned towards her mother, "I appreciate your helping me. It's hard getting away from everyone once they get going."

Tabitha Abernathy grinned as she patted her daughter's arm. "You have enough difficulties without having to deal with well-meaning people bombarding you."

"Thank you, Mother," Faith whispered in gratitude, knowing that though young and often mistaken for Faith's sister, she was as wise as women twice her age.

Faith's mother had been eighteen when she had married Thomas Abernathy. Less than a year later, they had their first child, Faith, and ten months after, Davis.

"Good morning, children," Pearl Abernathy

greeted with a sober expression as she joined her son's family in the front pew.

"Hello, Grandmother," Faith stated as she hugged the older woman, followed by the rest of the family.

Faith always marveled at how steadfast her grandmother appeared, even as her strawberry blonde hair grayed, and her green eyes hooded with painful memories of the past. Though she had lost her second son and only daughter over the past two decades, she remained strong in her faith and vigilant in her devotion to those that remained.

"Where is Grandfather?" Faith asked, looking around for the rough-and-tumble retired military man.

As if on cue, Mortimer Abernathy entered the church surrounded by the rest of the Abernathy children. Nancy and Ida were on either side of their grandfather, holding his hands, with Jack and Davis trailing behind.

"Good morning, everyone," Mortimer stated in a slow Southern drawl, as he took his hat off and sat in the pew with the family.

Though settled from his wild ways from many years ago in the military, Mortimer never took to the life of a plantation owner. He said it was because he had been born a second son and second sons were never meant to have to bear the burden. When he had returned from serving up in the North to find his brother had died from consumption, he was forced to run the family plantation for his mother. Though it had been a legacy handed down from his father, he had passed the mantle onto Faith's father as soon as he could.

It wasn't lost on Faith that her grandfather was a lingering relic from an era that was quickly fading away. Though deep into his sixth decade of life, Mortimer Abernathy was still a force to be reckoned with in South Carolina, and everyone knew it.

"Any news regarding Nathan's whereabouts?" Faith's grandfather asked with hope in his voice.

Faith shook her head, but couldn't muster a verbal reply. She prayed for a dose of her grandfather's hope and her grandmother's steadfastness along with protection for Nathan. Wherever he was and whatever he was going through, she knew he needed God to protect him.

Pastor Howell took to the pulpit, requesting everyone to stand to their feet with their hymnals. As the congregation sang, Faith let the melody cascade over her while the words of God's love and mercy filled her heart with peace.

CHAPTER 4

Imprisonment… it used to be a foreign notion to Nathan; however, over the past few weeks it had become an idea he held in contempt. The Union prison, or at least that was where he assumed he was being held, was little better than a place fit for rats.

At the moment, what he wouldn't give to be able to catch one and cook it. Food depravation was one of the means by which they tried to break Nathan, though it hadn't worked and he wouldn't let it. He would focus on what he must do to survive, returning to Faith, and leaving behind this awful place filled with awful men.

Try as he might, the conditions of his cell pressed Nathan to keep himself calm. Nathan was not a man who gave into darker feelings, but he was consumed by his anger towards the men who had been torturing him in an attempt to force him to give up Confederate secrets.

He didn't like the fact his captors could force him back to a place he had long forgotten. What if the rage devoured him? What if he could never put it back in the dark place he had shoved it long ago? If he returned broken, would Faith still love him? What if he never returned at all? Could she forgive him? Would she even know what happened to him, or would she be left to wonder? He loved her so much, he couldn't imagine her living with that hanging over her the rest of her life. He wasn't sure how he was going to do it, but he needed to get free and return to Faith.

Focusing on that purpose helped him fight off the shadows surrounding him. God still had plans for him, plans to prosper him, and not to harm him. The only thing capable of combating the darkness was his faith. His faith in God, his faith in his love for the woman he was going to marry, and his faith in the training he had received to never be broken.

The loud scrape of wooden chair legs interrupted Nathan's thoughts. Although aware his tormenter, Christopher, was in the room with him again, Nathan chose not to move but continue to look as if he was asleep.

"Come now, Nathan, I won't fall for any of your games again."

Nathan smiled inside, recalling the marks Christopher wore on the top of his hand, where the imprints of Nathan's teeth still lingered from their last encounter. Christopher had made the mistake of shaking Nathan out of his 'sleep' and was bitten for his trouble.

"Have it your way then, Nathan," he heard the other man state with an exasperated sigh.

The sound of a heavy, metal object being picked up from the ground across from him, echoed through the room. Nathan braced himself, not knowing what was coming but aware it would be nothing pleasant. He felt icy liquid hit him. The frigid coldness numbed his senses, but only for a moment. By the next second, the water stung like tiny needles of glass piercing every inch of his skin. Despite the pain, Nathan refused to react. It was what they wanted and expected of him. He wouldn't give them the satisfaction.

Moments ticked by as the room stayed motionless. No one made a move until Nathan raised his head, and through narrowed eyes, stared at the man standing across from him.

"Still nothing to say?" Christopher sighed with frustration and ran his hands through his thin, blond hair. He moved around and sat in the vacant chair across from Nathan.

"This would be easier if you gave in Nathan. You should consider it a compliment we want you enough to waste this much time on you."

Nathan was aware of his value to the other man. He would be an asset to their cause if they could convince him to turn against his country. However, they were dead wrong if they thought that would ever happen. "No, not me. They want my specialized set of skills and Confederate contacts, both of which I'll never give you."

"Nathan, I need to warn you, my bosses are contemplating other options of persuasion."

"You should know by now, I won't break. Nothing you do can make me turn against my country."

"Your loyalty should be the Union, to the United States of America, not some unorganized, zealous group of rebels who think themselves important enough to declare themselves sovereign. You should know better than anyone, the Union will never allow them to break from the rest of the country."

"I can see you're afraid of what we're capable of, of what we can and have done. You wouldn't be trying to convince me to turn against the Confederacy if that wasn't the case."

"You're mistaken," Christopher corrected with a shake of his head. "I'm simply trying to put an end to this ridiculous conflict as quickly as possible. Too many good men have died over the South holding onto an antiquated way of life. Help me end this, Nathan, before anyone else has to die."

"I will never help you," Nathan denied with resolve. "You have two choices; release me or kill me."

"There is a third choice. One you will not like." Christopher threatened, leaning forward but just out of reach. "If you don't accept our invitation to join us Nathan, we'll visit that little hole of a town —what's it called again—ah, yes, Myrtle Grove. If we can't have you, we will take your fiancée's oldest brother, Davis, instead."

"You won't touch him!" Nathan spat out in rage, struggling against the ropes that bound him. "I swear if any of you come near the Abernathy family, I'll make you—"

Christopher cut Nathan off mid-threat. "There's the man I've been waiting to see. Your true self has finally emerged. Welcome back, Lieutenant Maddox."

With a shake of his head, Nathan insisted, "Never. I'll never be that man again."

"It's your choice, but if you refuse our demands, we will go get the boy." Christopher paused and rubbed his beard. "If you agree to what we are asking, however, we could choose not to bother with him. We'd rather have a seasoned spy than spend the time training a new one. I don't think you want that for the boy either, considering you know what that entails."

Nathan's blood ran cold at the threat. He loved Davis like his own brother, and couldn't let him go through the awful experiences he did in order to be cultivated as a spy. The mind games and tactics would break the tender spirit of Davis.

Christopher stood up, walked over to the door, and opened it wide. He turned back and faced Nathan a final time. "I will give you the night to think on it. If you don't agree by morning, one of my men will make a trip to Myrtle Grove."

CHAPTER 5

A pang of sadness hit Faith as she looked around the table at her family's dejected faces. Two singular candles in plain tin pans lit the area, the conservation of the candles being a necessity nowadays. The long wooden table (the final remnant of their former luxurious life before the war) was sparse, with only a few plates, utensils, and glasses to use. All of the family's finer possessions including the china, silver, crystal and paintings, had been sold off to help offset the plantation's losses.

The worst of it had been when her mother had to part with her jewelry. She had cried as she handed them over to Thomas, saying she'd had the pearl necklace since he had given it to her on their first anniversary. Most of it was gone now, with only a few heirloom pieces they had hidden away in case Union soldiers or deserters found their way onto their land again.

Prior to Nathan's disappearance, joy and laughter still filled Sunday meals, despite the war being at the back of all their minds. Since the loss of Nathan, however, the silence was stifling.

Besides prayers for the meal, the only words spoken now at mealtime were "will you please pass the so-and-so" and "thank you." Although Nathan's empty chair was a permanent reminder of his absence, no one wanted to discuss it.

It had been this way ever since they received the letter informing them of Nathan's status. Not only was he Faith's fiancé, but he had become part of the family. When he had first come to Myrtle Grove looking for work, her father had offered him a job as a plantation hand.

Faith's attraction to Nathan had been immediate, though unexpected. He was handsome with thick dark hair, gorgeous blue eyes, and a tall, chiseled physique. Beyond his looks, his disposition was impressive too. He showed kindness to everyone and his faith in God radiated from him.

She could remember when they shifted from a

friendship to a romantic relationship, despite the difference in their stations.

Nathan was behind the house at the water spigot washing up for the evening meal. It had been a hot day. He was attempting to remove the sweat from his neck and face but was struggling.

Faith walked over to Nathan's side. "Here, take this." She extended the clean towel she had taken from one of the servants. As he looked at her with an irresistible, lopsided grin, her heart quickened and she felt like she would faint away on the spot

"Thank you," the simple words so powerful when uttered in his deep voice that they penetrated to her very core.

As his hand brushed her own, electricity shot up her arm, making her entire body tingle with excitement. He must have sensed it, too, because instead of removing his hand, he let it linger a moment longer than necessary.

Faith smiled back at him as her heart beat so rapidly she thought it would jump from her chest. She realized in that moment, he saw her for the first time as more than a friend.

Nathan worked hard and was dependable, quickly rising through the ranks at the plantation until he was promoted to foreman. Soon, he was taking on more and more responsibilities, even helping the family around the home with personal tasks. The more time Faith and Nathan spent together, the deeper their feelings grew, yet neither of them took the step to act on those feelings until one day they found themselves alone in the stable.

Nathan was returning one of the horses as Faith entered the stable for her afternoon ride. He finished latching the stall before turning to her with a look she had never seen in his eyes before.

"Is something wrong?" Faith inquired with concern.

"Yes, Faith, something is terribly wrong," Nathan declared with despair.

"What is it?" she asked, rushing to his side and placing her hand on his arm. "You aren't leaving Myrtle Grove, are you?"

The thought of never seeing him again was more than Faith could bear. She cared deeply for Nathan, she suspected she even loved him, and couldn't imagine living in a world where she didn't see him every day. She wished for more, but being a proper Southern woman, she knew it was not within her power to ask for it. She hoped in time, Nathan would make the leap and declare his affections, but the dream had yet to materialize.

If he had bad news, did it mean he had grown tired of living in a small town? He had lived in Mobile prior, and traveled all over the country as a soldier. Perhaps, he had decided he wasn't ready to settle down in one place. If that was the case, would Faith be able to accept him leaving?

"No, but there is a high likelihood that after I do what I plan to do tonight, I might be driven from this place."

Trepidation filled her heart as she pressed her lips together. Wringing her hands, she implored, "What are you going to do? Surely it can't be that dire."

"It depends on who you ask. Many might think it is," Nathan warned.

"Please, you cannot keep me in suspense," Faith asserted with frustrated concern.

Reaching out, he took Faith's hands in his own. "I'm going to ask your father for permission to marry you, Faith. Before I do though, I have to know if it's what you want."

"You should know by now, Nathan, I love you. I was just too scared to admit it because I wasn't certain how you felt, or how our lives will work together."

"I, too, have refrained for the same reason. I can't deny it any longer though. I love you, Faith, more than I ever thought possible." He pulled her towards him, bent his head until his lips met hers, and placed a kiss upon her mouth.

The intimate contact was searing. Her skin tingled all over, like a hot bath on a cold winter night. As he pulled her closer, he deepened the kiss, claiming her mouth for his own. In that moment, Faith knew she would never love another, and Nathan was her one and only.

True to his word, Nathan had asked for her hand in marriage. Her father had been surprised, but after Nathan laid out his plan of buying land and starting his own plantation, he convinced Thomas to trust him with his eldest daughter.

Nathan had kept money from his time in the military; along with the salary he had earned from working at Oak Haven, he had saved enough money to purchase twenty acres of land only miles from the Abernathy plantation.

Faith, along with her mother, and sister, Ida, had set about the time-consuming task of planning the wedding. It would be an elaborate affair, as any proper Southern woman's wedding from a respected family should be.

Nathan had been busy working on their home when he was conscripted. His military service interrupted his plans to have their home ready by their wedding. Their nearly-finished house was a constant reminder of what almost was and what might never come to be.

The clinking of forks against plates drew Faith's attention back to the present. She watched each of her siblings around the dinner table, noting how each of them was different. Davis was the first-born son, approaching eighteen, and attempting to step up and fill in for Nathan by taking on the majority of the work around the plantation. What worried Faith, along with the rest of her family, was that in a short time, her brother would be forced to join the war efforts when he turned eighteen. Davis, on the other hand, wanted to join and serve, but their father refused consent.

Faith remembered clearly the argument between the two of them regarding his desire to enlist.

"All you have to do is sign the papers, Father, and I can serve the confederacy and our family proudly."

"I've already lost one son to the war, I won't lose another. By law, the military can take you when you're eighteen, but until then, I will not consent."

"Do you know how that makes us appear? We look like cowards, Father. Is that what you want for the noble Abernathy name, to be remembered as cowards who refused to fight in the war for our country's independence?"

"No, but I will gladly live with that stigma if it means you live, too. I'm not signing those papers, and it's final," Thomas declared, crossing his arms in resolution.

The anger in Davis' eyes was clear, but he promised not to go against their father and sign-up anyway.

Determined as he was to join the war as a soldier, Faith knew Davis honored their father and wouldn't do it behind his back. The problem was, in just a few months, he would be eighteen and their father couldn't protect Davis any longer.

Faith knew her father had a deep-seeded need to protect Davis because he was unable to keep Nathan from the war and blamed himself over the loss of him. Though Faith believed Nathan was alive and would come home one day, the rest of the family had accepted the news and considered him dead. It was a hard pill to swallow that she was alone in her prayers and hope for Nathan's return, but she held fast to it none-the-less.

She supposed her own determination came from being the eldest child in the family. At nineteen, she was prepared to be a proper wife and mother and couldn't wait until she had the chance to start her own family. Her mother had trained her how to run a plantation household; along with learning how to manage servants and household routines, she had been schooled in the art of entertainment and conversation by the best tutors. Her mother had hoped for a good match for her, which was why Faith had been surprised when her father convinced her mother that Nathan was that match. Despite him being an orphan and a member of the lower class, her father saw the same thing in Nathan that she had. He was a good man, filled with resolve to make something of himself. He promised he would prove himself capable of living up to marrying an Abernathy woman, and she knew once he returned home, he would hold up to his word.

Jack was born after Davis. At thirteen, he was always getting into trouble, both at school (when it was still open) and by taking chances on the plantation. Just earlier that evening, Jack had gotten into trouble for putting a frog in Ida's apron. Ida came after Jack and was eleven. She loved helping in the house as well as watching Nancy, who rounded out the five children as the youngest. Ida was currently helping Nancy by cutting her food into smaller pieces.

As far as looks, Jack and Nancy took after their mother with brown hair and green eyes. Faith, Davis, and Ida resembled their father with blonde hair. Of the three, Faith was the only one who did not inherit their father's brown eyes, hers being green. Though they all were different from looks to personality, never had a family pulled together more than they had during the course of the war.

As workers disappeared one by one as they volunteered willingly to join the war or fled the area to avoid being conscripted, the Abernathys were left to work their own plantation for the first time in their lives. Their calloused hands, weathered skin, and tattered clothes were a testament to the fact.

Tonight, they ate a simple meal of cooked yams and their weekly ration of ham, both prepared by Tabitha and Ida who now handled all the chores of the main house. Faith, on the other hand, helped her brothers and father in the fields, determined to not let the war starve her family to death. Though the meal was meager, and three years ago Faith would have never dreamed of her family being reduced to squalor, she was thankful that at least all of them were alive and together.

Her eyes fell to the empty chair again, and she amended her previous thought. Almost all of them were together. Nathan was still missing, but she knew in her heart it wouldn't be forever.

After supper, everybody finished their final chores before bed. Faith cleared the dishes, carrying them into the kitchen and putting them in the wash basin. The kitchen, which had once worked well with a staff of three kitchen maids and a cook, now was larger than the family actually needed. They tended to only use the stove and two cabinets (out of dozens) for the minimal table settings and food they had on hand.

Faith said a prayer in silence as she worked, knowing that once she was done she could finally rest.

God, bring Nathan home safe to us. We miss him and our lives don't work without him. I know everything is possible through You, so Lord, please make a way.

After the final chores were finished, Faith climbed the long staircase that was now covered in stained, ragged carpet. Her hands, which used to glide along the smooth banister, now avoided it for fear she would add splinters to her already sore hands. Bare walls of the halls along the long route to her room on the second story made her home feel like a shell of its former glory; all of the paintings and decorations that once ordained the beautiful home were gone, either taken by the Confederacy to pay for the war or sold by the family for necessities.

She entered her bedroom, and for a moment, imagined how beautiful it once looked with her French-imported furniture and soft feather comforter and pillows. All of it had been sold and had been replaced by a singular bed and small dresser that once belonged to one of the servants. The small pieces of old, battered furniture made her room seem even smaller, but at the moment she didn't care.

Faith let her body fall onto the stiff bed, thankful that she at least didn't have to sleep on the floor—at least yet. As she drifted off to sleep, Nathan's smiling face filled her thoughts.

CHAPTER 6

Sleep evaded Nathan as he worried about the deadline. Part of him wondered if Christopher was bluffing, but Nathan had trained him to be ruthless and to never make empty threats. It would be just like him to abduct Davis and bring him here to torture in front of Nathan. He couldn't allow that to happen. The boy was too kind-hearted, making him the worst possible candidate to endure something of this nature. He would never survive. If torture broke even the strongest of men, Nathan knew it would destroy Davis.

"Nathan," a soft voice whispered in the blackness of his prison.

He turned his head to the side. Who was speaking to him?

"Listen, Nathan." The voice was quiet, yet strong, and came from nowhere but everywhere at once.

A warm hand touched his shoulder. "Do not fear. I will help you leave this place."

Within moments, the ropes disappeared, and he felt someone lifting him up. The stranger wrapped his arm around Nathan's waist, taking a majority of his weight. Despite his broken leg, the stranger guided Nathan towards the door.

"Who are you?"

"No time to talk," the voice whispered back. The sound was soothing to Nathan, despite where they were. Somehow, the voice prompted a peace in his heart he didn't understand.

As the door opened, the normal noise and light of the corridor disappeared. It was quiet, like a blanket of stillness had fallen upon the place, and once again, he couldn't see.

"Why should I trust you?" Nathan inquired, shaking away the peace and focusing on his training.

Suspicion was bred into him from his years as a spy. He worried this might be a trick to catch him off balance in hopes he would share the truth with the stranger, his rescuer. He didn't want to end up in a different room tied to another chair once they realized this new ploy didn't work.

"Someone who loves you sent me."

Nathan's mind was racing. Who knew where he was? Faith's family and their friends back in Myrtle Grove would do anything to find and save him. Though small and quirky, the town produced loyal neighbors who turned into faithful friends.

Nathan remembered during one of the first town meetings he attended, Mayor Bryant stood up and announced because of Nathan moving to Myrtle Grove, the population had officially reached 500 people. Everyone clapped and cheered as if it was the greatest accomplishment in the world. One week later, they held an ice cream social in the center of town to celebrate the milestone.

Unfortunately, even with so many devoted people trying to find him, he was aware the Union government never took chances with sensitive prisoners. He wasn't being kept in any official prison. Instead, he was held in a place in which no one should have been able to locate him.

"But I don't understand. Not that I'm ungrateful, but how did you find me?"

"The one who sent me can find anyone. Trust

me, Nathan. When we reach the outside, stay right by my side until I get you somewhere safe."

"I've little choice considering my current condition. But if you show untrustworthiness, I won't hesitate to do whatever it takes to get away."

As they reached another door, they paused long enough for the stranger to open it. The moonlight flooded Nathan's senses as he stepped out of the building. He took in a deep breath, inhaling his first lungful of fresh air in what must have been months.

"We need to keep moving. There is no time to stop."

He smelled the oak trees and felt the fallen leaves under his feet as they moved through the forest. Nathan tried to look around and make note of where he was, but no matter how hard he tried, he was unable to make out his surroundings or the details of the stranger helping him. Everything around him blurred.

"Where are we going?"

"Peter left Boston to find you. I'm taking you to him."

A chill shot up Nathan's back. No one besides Faith knew the man who had led him to the Lord lived in Boston.

"Wait, how do you know Peter?"

"As I've said, the one who sent me can find anyone, and He always helps the ones He loves."

Nathan was wondering about the cryptic answers he was getting from the stranger. "Who sent you to rescue me?"

The stranger didn't answer the question, but instead stated, "Just past this set of trees is a house on the edge of a clearing. Peter is inside and he is expecting you. He will take you back to your family."

"I don't understand."

"You will in time."

"None of this makes any sense," Nathan protested, frustrated he couldn't get his bearings or figure out what was going on.

"Faith is the evidence of things unseen."

"True, but I don't understand. This is happening so fast."

"You need to trust me," the stranger said in the same soothing voice as before.

The light was glowing from the window of the small cottage as they approached. Nathan stood on the doorstep and raised his hand to knock on the door. He hesitated for a moment, turning to thank his rescuer. Shocked, Nathan found the stranger gone. He looked everywhere but saw no trace.

He heard the door open and Peter's voice say, "He told me to be expecting you."

Nathan spun around and asked, "Who?"

"God."

CHAPTER 7

As Faith made her way down Main Street, she glanced at the list in her hand. Faith, along with Davis, was responsible for purchasing the weekly supplies at the Myrtle Grove General Store. They had just enough money to get the materials they needed for the garden, and groceries they didn't produce themselves. It wasn't much, but it would keep the family going for the next couple of weeks.

As Faith moved down the boardwalk, a man handed her a copy of The Index, a special newspaper created to feature the Confederacy war effort. There was a long article about the Confederate military strength along with a list of Southern victories. On the second page, there was a discussion of the right to self-govern and the need to resist oppression by the North. The article went on to say how it would be impossible to conquer the South due to the country's superiority in every aspect.

Faith folded up the newspaper and placed it in her bag so she could take it home and share it with the family. As she continued down the boardwalk, recruitment posters plastered the brick walls around town. Out of curiosity, she stopped to read one:

Your soil has been invaded by Abolitionist Foes, and we call on you to rally at once, and drive them back. We want volunteers to march immediately to Charleston and report for duty. Come one! Come all! And render the service due to your State and Country. Fly to arms, and succor your brave brothers who are now in the field.

Just a further bit down the road, another one read:

Action! Action! Should be our rallying motto, and the sentiment of Virginia's inspiring Orator, "Give me Liberty or give me Death," animate every loyal son of the Old Dominion! Let us drive back the invading foot of a brutal and desperate foe, or leave a record for posterity that we died bravely defending our homes and firesides—the honor of our wives and daughters—and the sacred graves of our ancestors!

Though Faith was a woman, the words resonated with her and made her want to stand behind her country. She could see why so many men were enticed by them to join the cause and fight against the tyranny of the North.

Remembering her task, Faith hurried along the boardwalk towards the butcher shop, hoping the rumors at church on Sunday were true. She couldn't remember the last time she had eaten beef and was hoping the shipment from the Charleston cattle company had indeed arrived.

The grin on Mrs. Brooks' face radiated as she entered the store. "Good morning, Faith, how are you doing this morning?"

Since she could remember, Mrs. Brooks had always stood behind the counter and taken care of the sales and display case. Mr. Brooks did the carving and butchering in the back, but poked his head out when someone came inside.

True to form, Faith saw Mr. Brooks' face appear from around the corner of the hallway. "How do you do, Faith?"

"Good morning, Mr. and Mrs. Brooks. I'm well this morning."

Faith felt relieved when they didn't bring up Nathan. She didn't feel like having to wade through one more person's condolences.

"What can we do for you?" Mrs. Brooks inquired.

Faith handed over the list. "Someone told me there is a shipment of beef today. Is there any left?"

Mrs. Brooks shook her head. "The meat never made it here. I found out that the meat was seized by a Union regiment and the entire shipment was lost."

Faith's cheerful expression vanished as the disappointment took hold. She shouldn't have gotten her hopes up, but she had thought about all the wonderful dishes she wanted to make with the meat. Baked beef and asparagus, pot roast with potatoes, beef stroganoff, and carrots with brisket of beef. Her mouth had salivated all the way to the shop, and now none of those tasty dishes were a possibility. The family would have to settle for less desirable types of meat, even if there was any of those to speak of.

"Do you have ham or sausages?"

"We have both, but the town conservation board has limited only a quarter pound of each per family."

There was no point in arguing; besides, she believed in the cause. Faith hoped their sacrifices would bring the men home shortly, maybe even perhaps Nathan.

Nodding, Faith stated, "We'll take both."

"I'll tell Theo what you need. I'll be back in a moment."

Faith picked through several of the pamphlets of recipes the shop offered that helped families manage meals with the limited supplies of food.

From behind her, a voice soared, "I thought it was you, Faith. I saw you through the window."

Turning to face her strawberry-blonde best friend, Faith smiled. "I was hoping I would run into you in town, although I'm surprised you could get away from Mrs. Richardson."

Hope Hammond snickered as she rolled her brown eyes. "I'm taking a short break. I must be back no later than ten." Hope lowered her voice as she leaned towards her friend in confidence. "You know how Mrs. Richardson can be."

Faith sure did. Mrs. Richardson acted as if their small library, which was actually just a moderate-sized room attached to the post office, was as grand as any library in a big city.

Two years ago, Faith had forgotten to return her library books on time by one day. Mrs. Richardson had given her a scorching rebuke. She never did it again.

"Are you free tomorrow after church? You can come to our place for lunch afterward," Faith offered.

Hope nodded. "I'd like that. Father isn't feeling well again."

Faith knew what that meant. Hope's father, Luke Hammond, was drinking again. He had been an officer with the Confederacy until he lost his leg during the war. Hope's older brother, Gregory, however, fared even worse. After being conscripted into the military only two months after his father returned home a cripple, Gregory died during the siege of Charleston during the second bombardment of Fort Sumter. Heavy artillery had thundered down on the entire region, and Gregory was one of the many casualties.

On top of all that, the Hammond plantation was failing. With several bad harvests, no workers, and little oversight, the place was close to the brink of ruin. Mrs. Hammond was doing what she could to help the plantation recover, but it was difficult without the support of her husband. Luke preferred to spend his time dwelling in the bottom of a bottle rather than help his family save their plantation. Hope did what she could, helping her mother at the plantation when she wasn't working at the library to cover the household costs.

Despite the immense struggles they faced, the Hammond women continued to maintain their strong faith. They were a true testament to the whole town.

"I'll see you tomorrow," Hope said, reaching out and giving a quick hug to her friend before taking off.

After the best friends separated and Faith paid for her items, she left the shop to find her brother. She saw Davis on the other side of the street talking to a man in uniform. Faith darted across the road and slowed as she came up to her brother's side.

"We're taking a few select soldiers who can be valuable in the right circumstance. You look like you're a mighty bright fellow and I have a man who can fix you up with the right papers so you can enter the war now. You won't need to wait until you're eighteen. All you need to do is—"

Faith reached out and grabbed Davis's arm. "We need to be getting to the general store, Davis. Come with me right now."

With an irritated look, her brother allowed Faith to lead him away.

"Father would have your head if he knew you wanted to join the military early. What were you thinking?" Faith chastised.

Davis responded in defense, "I'm thinking all my friends are already serving and I want to do my part. It's unfair that because I'm the youngest of my friends, I end up having to wait longer than all of them."

"Did you ever think it was what God intended? It's bad enough the military made Nathan return; now you want to join by choice. Nathan would be disappointed with that decision."

"Well, Nathan isn't here is he?" Davis stated resentfully.

Faith flinched at the statement. Although true, she didn't like how flippant her brother was about it.

He must have noticed her reaction because he apologized. "I'm sorry Faith, I didn't mean it. Please forgive me. You know how much I care for Nathan."

"If you do, stop being foolish about fighting in the war. You don't want Nathan to return to find you gone."

She could see in her brother's eyes he didn't have the same hope she did regarding Nathan's return. He didn't voice his feelings though, and instead said, "You win, Faith. I won't talk to those men anymore."

"Good. Glad to hear it." Patting her brother on the back, Faith changed the subject. "Let's go get the rest of the items on the list."

Davis nodded as they headed towards the next corner of Main Street.

CHAPTER 8

G roggy and disoriented, Nathan opened his swollen eye and saw his good friend and mentor looking at him.

"How long have I been out?" Nathan inquired, still confused from all that had happened to him.

"Two days. While you were asleep, I loaded you onto the wagon and moved you farther away to a safer location." Peter chuckled. "Did I mention, for a skinny fellow, you sure weigh a lot."

"Don't make me laugh. I hurt everywhere." With a shake of the head, Nathan stated with shock, "I still can't believe it's you."

"When God tells me to do something, I do it. He told me to come here and wait for you."

Nathan smiled as he thought about Peter

Hawarden's resourcefulness. After leaving the military's service, Nathan had wandered around the country for three months until he found a job on the Abernathy plantation in Myrtle Grove. One year later, he received a letter in the mail from Peter. Apparently, he had looked into his whereabouts so he could resume communication.

Sitting up, Nathan swung his legs over the side of the cot. The room began to spin and nausea took hold. For several moments, he focused on keeping the bile from coming up.

"Are you all right? Do you need me to get you a glass of water?" Peter asked with concern.

"I'm fine," Nathan grunted out. Forcing himself to raise his head, he looked around at the simple cottage composed of one giant room containing only a cot, a table with two chairs, and a fireplace. "Where are we?"

"I thought I should let you rest considering all you have been through," Peter stated with a concerned look. "The Union soldiers have expanded their search parameter which means by morning, this place will no longer be safe. We need to leave tonight."

"I still don't understand. How did you find where they were holding me? Who was the person who brought me to you? How did you convince them to help me?"

A bewildered expression settled on Peter's face. "What person? I've been here alone this whole time."

What did Peter mean? He had to have been behind the man who rescued him. Nothing else made sense.

"Did this person ever give a name?" Peter asked, tilting his head to the side with curiosity.

"No, the person was vague. I couldn't even get a straight answer any time I asked a question."

"Did you see your rescuer?" Peter probed further.

Nathan tried to remember the other night. It wasn't like him to ignore the details of any given situation, let alone a dangerous one. It was a spy's second nature to notice everything, yet he couldn't recall any specifics about the stranger.

"No, and I'm not sure why," he confessed with apprehension.

Peter walked over to the fire where a delicious smelling pot of food was cooking. Nathan's stomach twisted, growling with anticipation as Peter lifted the ladle and stirred the liquid. "Is it possible God didn't want you to see the stranger's face, or you wouldn't accept it if you did?"

Perplexed, Nathan furrowed his eyebrows together. "What do you mean by that?"

"There is the possibility God sent an angel to help you."

"Whoever helped me *was* an angel," Nathan nodded in agreement. "It's why I want to know who it is. I want to find him to thank him."

"That's just it, I'm not talking figuratively. Can't it be possible God sent an actual angel to rescue you? He did it for Peter and Paul in the New Testament of the Bible, which means there's a chance he did it for you the other day."

Three days ago, Nathan would have never thought it possible. He prided himself on being a realist. He didn't put much stock in supernatural beings like angels, so the possibility one rescued him seemed ludicrous. Yet, in his spirit, the likelihood resonated. As the disbelief melted away, Nathan admitted, "I can't believe I'm saying this, but you're right, Peter. God sent an angel to save me."

Peter handed him a bowl of stew along with a spoon. "Since we have that settled, we need to move onto more pressing matters. After you eat, we can figure a way of getting you back to Myrtle Grove."

"What is your suggestion?" Nathan inquired.

"We're going to smuggle you out of the North."

Two hours later, Nathan was praying for their safety while hiding in the back of Peter's wagon. Every bump and pothole in the road jolted Nathan as they sped through the back ways of Massachusetts. His body was still healing from the damage Christopher had inflicted on him, which made each impact more painful than the last. To make matters worse, he had several thick, wool blankets encompassing his body to keep him hidden. Although grateful for the shield they provided, they were stifling, making it hard to breathe. The blankets also created a thick layer of disgusting sweat which covered his body.

Nathan kept telling himself, if he made it through this, he would return to Faith and marry her. He didn't care if the house was finished, or if the war was still raging on around them, he was going to marry the woman he loved and give her the life she deserved.

"How are you holding up back there?" Peter shouted.

After patting the seat, Nathan waited, too mindful of his surroundings to utter a word.

"I'll take that as you mean you're doing fine."

Good. Peter got the point. Nathan was tired and didn't want to yell through the stuffy blankets.

Several more minutes went by before the vehicle slowed to a stop. Was it another checkpoint? Every time they passed one, his stomach clenched in fear. He knew if Union soldiers found, Nathan would be returned to the black pit he had just escaped. What worried him more was what would happen to Peter. They would consider him a Southern sympathizer and kill him on the spot.

Nathan said a silent prayer as he waited under the blankets. *Lord, please help us to get through the check-point. Keep us safe and help me get back to Faith.*

"It's rather late for you to be traveling alone out here. Where are you going?" Nathan heard a gruff Bostonian accent inquire.

"I'm delivering supplies to the fort at Salisbury Point," Peter stated.

"I need to see your papers authorizing this travel," the other man demanded.

"Here you go."

Several seconds ticked by before the Union soldier probed further, "What's in the wagon?"

"My luggage, several bags of rice, two bushels of potatoes, and some fresh apples for the soldiers. The blankets are to keep the bugs from them during the travel." Nathan could feel him shift items in the wagon, and remembered the plan included revealing the baskets of food. "I'm a pastor out of Boston and my church collected donations to help the soldiers."

There was another long pause as the soldier poked around the wagon, several times coming close to making contact with Nathan. His hands bawled into fists at his side, preparing to strike if the final blankets were removed to reveal his location. Nathan wouldn't go back to prison, which left him only one option, fight or die.

"Thank you for your contributions to the war effort, Mr. London. You're free to go."

The wagon lurched forward, and they were back on the road. Nathan sighed with relief. Apparently, Peter's story and alias did the trick and the Union soldier believed him. Soon, Nathan would be home in Myrtle Grove with his beloved Faith.

CHAPTER 9

After deciding she wanted to bake a dessert to cheer up the family, Faith pulled out the new recipe she had found in a war pamphlet called "Molasses Apple Pie," which she planned to share at the town's next recipe swap night. She gathered the ingredients she would need, including the molasses her neighbors produced by crushing sugar cane with wooden rollers moved by horse power. The juice was then boiled in giant wash pots, cooled, and finally stored in jars. The process was called "long sweetening" and the resulting substance could be used in place of sugar, which was in shortage because of the war. Faith was grateful they had enough to trade with her family for some of their squash harvest.

She placed the freshly made crust onto the bottom of the pie pan, then arranged the sliced, green apples—purchased from the local orchard outside of Myrtle Grove—into the pan, sprinkled nutmeg and cinnamon over the apples, and added the required molasses. She covered it with a lattice crust top and placed it in the wood-burning oven near the hearth.

As the pie heated, the house filled with the delicious smell of baking apples while Faith cleaned up. A knock sounded from the front of the house, causing Faith to pat her hands against her apron and call out, "Be there in a moment."

As she opened the door, her mouth fell wide in astonishment and her heart raced with joy. Nathan stood across the threshold. His body exhibited visible wounds along with a leg that was bandaged up. He had a crutch under one arm and dark circles under his eyes, but otherwise he appeared intact.

Rushing towards him, Faith buried herself in his waiting embrace as tears streamed down her cheeks. "Oh, Nathan, I'm so glad you're home!" Her body was shaking and she felt like she would pass out from the sheer shock of seeing him again.

His chin rested on top of her head as he whispered, "It's good to have you back in my arms, Faith."

"I've prayed for this every day." She wanted to say more but her throat was constricted by emotion. She had hoped and believed he would return home, but nothing prepared her for the simultaneous sensations of relief and elation she was experiencing. She basked in the familiar strength of his arms which encircled her. Her cheek rested against his chest, the recognizable rhythm of his heartbeat melodic to her ears. Wanting to take care of him, Faith leaned back and inquired, "How are you? What do you need? Something to eat? Something to drink?"

As he shook his head, he stepped back and leaned against the doorframe of the house. He appeared detached, his attention fixated on something beyond where they were. After a moment, he focused and looked at her dirty attire. Faith blushed with embarrassment. "I imagined looking in better shape than this when you came back home."

His eyes shot to hers as he professed, "Never think it. You're the most gorgeous sight I've ever seen."

She laughed, rebuffing his statement. "You must still be delirious from your whole ordeal. I haven't had the pleasure of wearing a soiled-free dress in months." Faith wasn't good at taking compliments. She changed the subject by inquiring, "Why didn't the military inform me they found you?"

"Because they didn't find me. Someone else did."

Questions formed and accumulated in Faith's head. When she could wait no longer, she blurted out, "What happened? Who found you? Why did the military assume you were dead?"

She could hear the weariness in Nathan's voice as he responded, "Can we sit down first?"

What was she thinking? Whatever he went through, he sounded exhausted and didn't need her hammering him with questions.

Faith grabbed his hand and led him into the house. "Let's go into the parlor."

They made their way into the once opulent room that had been filled with expensive solid wood furniture, rich tapestries, and beautiful oil paintings. All of it was gone now, with only a couple of chairs and a sofa to fill the large room. Though it was sparse, Faith didn't care. All that mattered was Nathan had returned. The rest could be replaced once the war was over.

Nathan's eyes settled upon her face, but after a

few moments, his vision clouded and distance overtook him again.

"Tell me where you were, what happened to you," Faith pleaded, wanting to understand why she had been led to believe he was dead.

"I'm not at liberty to divulge the details, but before I could complete my final mission, the Union soldiers set an ambush and took me prisoner."

Faith was in disbelief. "The Northerners held you captive this whole time?"

"Yes, they grabbed me two weeks after the last letter I sent."

"What did they want from you?"

"They wanted to persuade me to switch sides."

She brushed her fingertips down his arm, touching the marks and scars that riddled his body, evidence of their persuasion. It hurt her to just see the scars on his handsome physique; she couldn't even imagine how painful it must have been for him to endure them. "Do they still hurt?"

"Not as much as it did at first. I'm healing every day, and in a few months, the doctors assure me I will be mended, all but my leg that is. I will have a permanent limp because of the break not being treated in the beginning."

"How awful," Faith whispered with dismay. "I can't believe someone could do this to you."

"It's in the past, and what's important is that I came home to you. I don't want to talk about what they did to me anymore."

Wanting to respect his wishes, Faith focused on something else. "You mentioned someone found you? Who was it?"

Faith noticed Nathan squirmed in his seat and averted his eyes before he answered. "Peter was the one who helped me get home."

"Peter Hawarden? The man who helped you become a Christian? The one who writes you often? How did that happen?"

Nathan nodded. "He helped me cross the Northern border and made sure I connected with the Confederate military in Virginia. He risked so much to help me; I can never repay him."

Curious about how Peter found him, Faith inquired, "How did he know where you were?"

"He says God told him."

Faith sucked in a deep breath and held it for several seconds before she whispered, "I've heard of God orchestrating such feats. God must have special plans for you, Nathan, for Him to go to such lengths to see you home safely." Another question popped into Faith's head. "Where is Peter now? I should like to thank him for saving your life."

"He had to return to his home in Boston. He told me to give you his best."

Faith was disappointed she wasn't going to get to meet the man who had been so important to Nathan. Peter had been like a brother to the man she loved, and she would have appreciated knowing more about Nathan from before he was in Myrtle Grove. Wanting only to dwell on the happy return of the man she loved, Faith said, "Apparently, I owe a debt of gratitude to Peter now." With a slight laugh, she added, "We may have to name our first child after him."

"I'm grateful every day God sent Peter to help me. But now that I'm back, being home with you is all that matters. I don't want to dwell on the past." Nathan placed his hand on the side of her face and rubbed his thumb along the edge of her cheek. "I love you, Faith. Your love kept me alive."

He leaned forward and placed his lips upon hers. The warmth from it spread through her and she realized, she didn't want him to ever stop kissing her again.

The moment was perfect before a rush of shouts and squeals interrupted as the Abernathy family piled in for the mid-day meal.

"It's so good to see you Nathan!" Davis shouted, rushing up and slapping his friend on the shoulder, who flinched slightly from the contact.

"Welcome home," Ida stated.

Jack nodded towards Nathan. "Happy you're back."

"We were so worried," Faith's mother proclaimed with a soft smile.

"The plantation hasn't been the same without you," Faith's father asserted in his matter-of-fact way. "We can finally start running smoothly again now that your home."

The only one who remained quiet was Nancy, who had tears forming in the corners of her eyes. "They told us you were dead!" She ran from the room crying. Footsteps could be heard scurrying up the stairs, and a few moments later, a door slammed shut.

"Don't worry about Nancy. She doesn't understand, and it's overwhelmed her. I'll go speak with her," their mother offered, heading out of the parlor.

Faith watched as everyone talked to Nathan and gave him hugs. He was responding in the ways he should, but Faith felt as if there was an invisible wall keeping him from engaging with the family. She wasn't sure what happened, but something had drastically changed in the man she loved.

CHAPTER 10

Nathan had wanted to go talk to Nancy himself, knowing they had a special bond. The girl had latched onto him when he first started spending time with the Abernathy family, following him around everywhere. In turn, he had doted on her and given her particular attention. However, since returning, the feelings emanating from the Abernathys hadn't overwhelmed only her. He didn't know how to handle the emotions either.

His despondency stemmed from how he had handled the interrogations and beatings. Once the torture became too much for him to bear, he had turned off his emotions. It was better to feel nothing than the pain inflicted. He wasn't sure how to turn them back on now that he was home. He was trying, and at certain times, he could almost glimpse the man he used to be until something pricked his memory of his captivity, catapulting him straight back into the dark abyss of nothingness.

Nathan sat around the table with the people he cared most about in the world, but he couldn't muster any joy. It had been his dream to return to his life in Myrtle Grove. He was back, but wondered if the biggest part of his soul would stay in the derelict Union prison. His body might have escaped; however, the rest of him remained trapped there.

After dinner, he excused himself from the table and made his way onto the porch. He needed a moment to himself where he didn't feel he had to perform for everyone around him.

"How are you doing, Son?" Mortimer asked, as he came out on the veranda and patted the younger man's back. When Nathan didn't respond, Mortimer continued, "You know, I served in the United States Army when I was about your age. I had no idea how hard it was going to be to take another man's life. I was just following orders, but from the first bullet to the last bullet, it never got easier, and I spent the better part of a decade running from the memories. I know it's not the same, what you went through, but I do know that I don't want you to waste as many years as I did avoiding dealing with the past.

Nathan was surprised by Mortimer's confession. He was usually a man of few words, divulging little of anything about his past. "Thank you, Mr. Abernathy, for sharing that with me. I want to find a way to let go of what I went through. I'm just not sure how."

"You need to give it—all of it—to God. If you do that, He will carry that burden for you. He has for me."

Their somber conversation was interrupted by a peal of laughter from behind them as Nancy and Jack came spilling out of the house.

"Tag. You're it!" Nancy squealed as she poked her brother and took off running out into the garden.

"Not fair, Nancy, I wasn't ready," Jack whined as he darted through the hedges, trying to find his sister.

Evading him, she teased with laughter, "You can't get me. I'm right here. Come get me, Jack."

Nathan watched as the youngest Abernathy children chased each other around the garden. One day he hoped he would do the same with his own children he would have with Faith. If he was ever to make his relationship work with her, he was going to have to find a way to make peace with his past.

He sent up a silent prayer for God to help him let go of what happened to him, and find a way to live his life again.

◈

Two weeks crawled by, and Nathan hadn't found a way to fit back into his old life. He had tried to dodge spending time with anyone, knowing he was poor company. Several times he had been curt with Faith and her family, unable to gather the ability to pretend for long periods of time. He tried to control it, but angry words kept spilling out before he could stop them.

Faith didn't deserve the hostile treatment; none of the Abernathys did. Nathan knew it, and he wanted to do better, but he couldn't figure out how. He knew he should be happy to be home where he was free again. For months, he had been faced with oppressive restriction, but he still couldn't connect to his old life.

Today, as he walked into church, he could feel the urge to flee nipping at the back of his mind.

The sea of smiles and concerned looks were overwhelming, causing Nathan to avert his eyes from the other church parishioners. He had avoided coming to church until Faith commented on his sudden reclusive nature. Against his better judgment, he forced himself to head into the town with the family to prove to her that he was adjusting.

Nathan used to enjoy attending church on Sundays. Pastor Howell would often give a message about love, forgiveness, or an array of other diverse, relevant, and inspiring topics. Each time, he learned something new that he could use in his own life. Now, all he wanted to do was hide away in the bunkhouse of the plantation and never step foot in town again.

As Nathan sat down in the Abernathy family pew, he looked over at Faith, wondering what she was thinking. Her kindness and understanding seemed limitless since he had come home; however, it was clear she was concerned about him.

Faith should be. He worried about himself. It wasn't like him to dwell in despondency. He had always succeeded at forcing away unwanted emotions, focusing on the task at hand instead. It was what had made him such an effective spy.

This time, try as he might, the negative feelings

in the pit of his stomach overshadowed everything, despite how hard he prayed for it to be otherwise.

As Pastor Howell took to the pulpit, Nathan tried to concentrate on the message.

"Good morning, everyone. I'm grateful to see each of you, including our long absent friend and neighbor, Nathan Maddox." Pastor Howell looked at Nathan as he continued in his slow Southern drawl, "We prayed for your safe return and God answered our prayers. We're glad you're home."

The church members' unexpected attention made Nathan want to fidget in his seat. He disliked the attention, but followed social protocol by responding with a wave and smile.

The service passed by while the hollow feeling in the center of Nathan gnawed at him. He tried to listen, but something was keeping him from doing so. His mind drifted back to his time in the Union prison, not allowing him to concentrate on anything else but how much of himself he had lost in that place.

As Pastor Howell concluded the service, Nathan attempted to leave the church without notice, hoping to get away from everyone before being detained. He had no such luck as he heard from behind him, "Good morning, Nathan," from a deep male voice. He turned to find Mr. And Mrs. Brooks standing behind him.

"We're so glad you're home," Mrs. Brooks stated with a warm smile. "Faith never gave up hope you were alive. She's a strong woman and you're lucky to have her."

"I know I am, Mrs. Brooks," Nathan said in agreement. "Faith is the reason I'm still alive."

His eyes flickered to the exit as he contemplated how to get away. He felt like the walls of the church were closing in on him and at any moment he was going to blow up if he had to stay there one more moment.

"Now that you're back, I'm sure you'll be finishing up the house and a wedding will be on the horizon," Mr. Brooks stated with a hint of question in his tone.

"That's the plan," Faith confirmed as she arrived next to Nathan, placing her arm through his.

Without being able to help it, Nathan stiffened under her touch. Unanticipated physical contact still jarred him after all the abuse he sustained while imprisoned.

Faith's eyes darted towards him with a shocked look of hurt as she pressed her lips together. A moment later, she dropped her arm from his and turned to face the couple standing beside them.

"We should probably be on our way. The rest of the family is waiting," Faith explained, but Nathan could tell she was making an excuse to help him escape.

Mr. Brooks reached out and shook Nathan's hand. "If you need any help, you come on by the butcher shop. I'm more than willing after all you have done for our country."

With a curt nod, Nathan responded, "Thank you."

Once the Brooks departed, Faith turned her attention to Nathan. "I meant to stay by your side the whole time but Bonnie stopped me. She wouldn't let me go until I answered all her questions."

"You didn't need to rescue me," Nathan admonished, not liking the idea of Faith coddling him.

Faith raised an eyebrow as she tilted her head, looking at him as if she didn't understand why he was so upset. "I wanted to keep you from getting bombarded with too much attention all at once. I know how hard this must be for you."

"No, you don't know, Faith. I wish you would

quit trying to act like you know what I need. I don't need your protection. I'm not broken," he snapped as he stepped away from her, trying to put some distance between them.

A look of pain crossed Faith's face before she shook her head and defended, "I never said you were."

Nathan heard the harshness in his own words but couldn't stop more from bursting from his mouth. "Well, you're acting like it, and I don't want you, or anyone else for that matter, to treat me with kid gloves."

"I don't know what you're talking about," Faith cried out in frustration, as tears crept into the corner of her eyes. "I've done nothing but love you." Glancing around the church as if worried someone overheard their argument, she quickly added, "I need a moment to myself."

Nathan watched as Faith rushed from the church. He wanted to reach out and stop her, to pull her around, and tell her he loved her too. He should have but he didn't; he couldn't.

"Good morning, Nathan."

With an internal sigh, he stiffened at the sound of Pastor Howell's voice behind him. He wondered how much the other man had heard. Just what

Nathan needed, a lecture about his behavior towards Faith. He braced himself as he turned around ready for a reprimand.

"I was wondering if you would mind coming by later this week to talk."

Nathan's eyebrows came together in a furrow of confusion. "What do you want to discuss?"

"I hope to go over a few matters with you, get your opinion on ideas I have for the volunteer committee for the war effort."

Nathan worried he would want to talk about his captivity which Nathan refused to do. Just the thought of doing that made him break out in a sweat and his chest palpitate. "I can come by, but I want to make sure you're aware I can't discuss the details of my assignment in the war."

A knowing look crossed Pastor Howell's face as he nodded. "You have my word I won't pry for information."

Before Nathan could make his getaway, Davis sauntered up with his hands in his pockets.

"Do you have a moment?"

Had Davis witnessed Nathan's behavior towards his sister? If he had, it would explain why Davis wanted to speak with him. As her brother, he was protective of Faith, defending her at every opportunity. It had taken Davis several months to warm up to the idea of Nathan courting his sister. Diligently, Nathan had worked to win over Davis's approval. Once Nathan showed he not only cared for Faith, but could provide for her and take care of her in a worthy manner, Davis relaxed and accepted their engagement. Nathan hoped he hadn't caused Davis to distrust him again by his earlier conduct with Faith.

"What can I do for you, Davis?"

"I saw Faith run out of here upset. You have any idea why?"

Even as Davis asked the question, Nathan was certain he already had formed an assumption in his head. He just wanted Nathan to confirm his suspicion.

Nathan toughened under the scrutiny, forcing himself to not sound defensive. "We had a bit of a disagreement. It was nothing."

"It didn't look like nothing. What were you arguing about?" Davis probed, and though his question sounded casual, there was a hint of disappointment in his tone.

There was no point in trying to hide the truth. Davis would just keep pestering Nathan until he answered him. With a heavy sigh, Nathan revealed what happened. "She was trying to handle me like a child. I told her to stop."

"You might want to give her a little slack. Your time away has been hard on her and nobody really knows how to handle any of this." Davis placed his hand on his friend's shoulder and squeezed it. "She loves you, Nathan, and her belief in you has been unwavering, but even a strong woman can be pushed too far. If you don't want to lose her, you need to figure out a way to stop hurting her." Without another word, Davis turned around and headed out the door, leaving Nathan to contemplate his friend's warning.

CHAPTER 11

Faith's heart dropped into her stomach as tears slipped down her cheeks. In all the time she had known Nathan, he never had shown such mean behavior with anyone, let alone her. There were a few incidents when he had become short with the family since returning, but nothing like this latest outburst.

She understood he didn't want to talk about what happened. It was clear from the way he would change the subject to avoid talking about the war. What she didn't expect or understand was why he got angry with her just now. All she had wanted to do was help him, but instead, she made him mad at her.

Faith had been so resolute in her belief that

once he came home everything would return to normal. How could she be so mistaken? She had been naïve to never contemplate the possibility that their relationship might not survive the ramifications of the war and what it did to Nathan.

Faith leaned against the giant oak tree outside the church. She tried to calm herself by saying a silent prayer to God. *Lord, please help me to understand what is going on with Nathan. I don't want to upset him and I know he has been through a lot. I ask for Your guidance during this trying time. Show me how to be what he needs.*

Hope bounced up to Faith beaming. "Good morning, Faith, I wanted to invite you and Nathan to come over for dinner." Hope must have realized something was wrong because she tilted her head to the side and inquired, "What's going on Faith? You look upset."

Not wanting to involve anyone else, Faith shrugged. "Nothing I can't handle."

"Are you sure you don't want to talk about it?"

Even though Faith wanted to ask Hope's opinion, she refused to paint Nathan in a poor light. After all he had been through, he didn't deserve to have people pass judgment on him.

"It doesn't matter. It's only temporary, anyhow."

Faith felt like she was trying to convince Hope

as much as herself. She hoped it was fleeting. Nathan had been acting peculiar since his return, secretive and distant. She knew he must have survived awful experiences while being held captive. She wished he would confide in her, not about the details, but at least how it affected him. Instead, he kept it all inside himself.

What if Nathan couldn't handle the experiences he had? Would it mean he would end up like Hope's father? Mr. Hammond not only punished himself, but everyone around him, for what the war had done to him and his son. If that was the case, maybe even though Nathan had returned, she might have lost him anyway.

Faith didn't feel like being with anyone else right now, and wasn't even sure if Nathan would be willing to go with her. "Can we come for dinner another day, Hope?"

The disappointment in her friend's eyes made Faith instantly regret rejecting the offer.

Hope forced a smile as she nodded. "Of course, it's just Father is having a good day which means we can have visitors. I understand though; perhaps another time."

"Here you are Faith. Mother wants to get back to Oak Haven and sent me to find you." Davis looked from Faith to Hope. With a lopsided grin, he added, "It's good to see you, Hope."

A blush covered her friend's entire body as she smiled at Davis. "I'm glad to see you, too. Are you coming into the library again this week?"

Faith's head jerked towards her brother as she gave him a questioning look. Since when did he go to the library? As far back as Faith could remember, Davis had hated reading.

"I sure am, Hope. I'll return my books about growing crops and pick up a new one about fertilization techniques."

Even though the topics made sense, Faith suspected if he was going to the library, it wasn't for the books. He had never paid much attention in school and reading had been his least favorite subject. Was her brother interested in her best friend?

"I'll put a couple aside for you," Hope promised with a smile and a twinkle in her eye.

"Thanks. I'll let you two finish up and tell the family you'll be ready to go soon, Faith."

As her brother sauntered off, Faith wondered what she had just witnessed. Neither one of them had told her Davis had been going into the library, which made her wonder if they had been hiding their interactions. Was there something going on between them that they didn't want anyone to know about?

Before Faith could question her friend, Hope gestured towards her mother who was standing at the bottom of the steps. "I have to go. Mother and I need to get home so we can make dinner."

Faith watched as her friend walked over to join her mother, before turning to face the tree. She found the spot where hers and Nathan's initials were carved into the trunk.

F.A.

+

N.M.

As she traced her finger along the edges, Faith thought back to when they first had put them there. They had wanted their relationship to stand the test of time, like all the other sets of initials which sprinkled the tree's trunk.

It had become an unofficial tradition for couples to sneak into the church courtyard at night. They would make promises of how they would love each other forever, under the covers of the moonlight and twinkling stars. Life was simple before the war broke out in America. Everything changed in Myrtle Grove because of it, and now, she wasn't even sure if her relationship with Nathan would survive.

"I remember when we carved those."

Faith glanced over her shoulder, but avoided making eye contact with Nathan, still hurt from his earlier behavior. She didn't want to reminisce with him after the way he treated her.

"My parents are ready to go. We should head over to them," Faith stated as she moved towards the pathway which led from the church grounds.

Nathan stretched out his hand and stopped Faith from leaving. "I'm sorry about the way I acted. You didn't deserve my mistreatment. Coming home has proven more difficult than I had expected and I haven't been handling it well." He pulled her towards him and wrapped his arm around her waist. "Will you please forgive me?"

Faith gazed into his eyes and saw the sincerity of his plea. She couldn't stay angry at him, even if she had wanted to. Nodding, she stated, "You know I will. I love you."

"And I love you, too." Letting her go, he leaned against the tree as he glanced over at Hope. "What were you two talking about?"

"She asked if we would come over today for dinner."

"What was your answer?"

"Under the circumstances, I thought it would be best if we declined the invitation."

She could tell by his expression he was contemplating what to do. After a few seconds ticked by, he shrugged. "If it's important to you, we can go over."

Her eyebrows shot up in surprise. "You would be all right with going?"

"Consider it my peace offering," he stated with a grin.

Faith smiled back at him. "Thank you. Let me go tell Hope."

Grateful for the turn of events, she knew it was a sign from God to not give up on Nathan. If he was willing to do something that made him uncomfortable just to make her happy, then he was trying to make things right between them. The least she could do is make the same effort in return.

CHAPTER 12

"It's so good to see you both," Joanna Hammond proclaimed as she opened the door and gestured for them to enter their home. "Come in, come in."

It was obvious the house had recently been cleaned. There wasn't a speck of dust anywhere and the large home smelled of lemons. Like Faith's family, the Hammonds had come from a long legacy of plantation owners, but along with Mr. Hammond's leg and son, the war had taken most of their plantation too. The crops failed with no one to tend to them, and if they weren't able to find a way to start producing again, they would lose their family home and land.

"When Hope told me you could make it, I was

glad to hear it. I think it will do Luke good to have company, especially someone with a similar history."

Nathan realized Mrs. Hammond was hoping her husband could relate to Nathan and form a bond over their experiences in the war. What she didn't realize was Nathan was sure neither of them wanted to talk about it. It was easier to avoid the subject, but of course civilians didn't understand that.

Hope's mother gestured towards the dining room. "Why don't you both sit down at the table. Hope and I are finishing up in the kitchen."

Faith and Nathan made themselves comfortable, taking their seats around the table. A few moments later, Luke Hammond entered the room hobbling on one leg with a crutch under his arm to keep his balance. Mr. Hammond's frown showed his displeasure over their presence.

"I see my wife and daughter are at it again. They dragged someone else home hoping to force me to make peace with the war."

Nathan ignored his barb, stood up, and moved around the table until he was next to Mr. Hammond. He extended his hand, saying, "I don't think we have met Mr. Hammond. You were already serving when the military conscripted me. I'm Nathan Maddox. It's an honor to meet you, sir."

"Believe me, son, it's no honor to meet me," the other man slurred out in anger. From his bloodshot eyes, and the stench of liquor permeating from his pores, it was clear Mr. Hammond was drunk. "I was prideful and foolish when I rushed off to serve in the war. By the time I realized what I'd done, it was too late to rectify the poor decision. I tried to make the best of it, figuring I could survive the war while serving my country. Unfortunately, I lost my leg because of my stupidity and misplaced loyalty. The military wasn't happy to stop there though; they decided they needed to take my Gregory too. Now I'm a—"

Mrs. Hammond walked into the room and interrupted, "Now that's enough, Luke. We have guests and you need to stop right now."

"I don't have to do any such thing, Joanna," Mr. Hammond snapped. "This is my house and you best remember that."

"I'm aware, Luke, but we do have guests," Mrs. Hammond pointed out in a kinder tone.

From the sour look on his face, it was clear he wanted to object. Hope entered and kneeled down next to him. "Please, Father, can you refrain from behaving this way while my friends are here?"

With an exasperated sigh, he relented. "I supposed I can hold my tongue for the time-being. Let's get on with it then." Mr. Hammond moved to the head of the table. He took his seat, then handed his plate to his wife. Once he was served, he shoveled his food into his mouth. Apparently, there was no grace to be said in the Hammond home.

Mrs. Hammond and Hope conversed with Nathan and Faith while Mr. Hammond ate in silence. His lack of interaction made it clear he was only allowing them to stay to appease his wife and daughter.

As Nathan watched him, he wondered if that was his future? If he continued to let his time in the war affect his present life, would he give up his chance for happiness? Nathan didn't want to end up like the bitter, angry man sitting across from him. Luke Hammond was so overtaken by the losses of his past he couldn't see the blessings he still had.

"Everyone wait here. I'll get dessert." Hope exited the dining room and went into the kitchen.

"We're glad you could join us Nathan." Mrs. Hammond poured cups of coffee in preparation for dessert, then handed them to each of her guests. "What are your plans since returning from the war?"

"I suppose I'll just pick up where I left off. I'm still adjusting to civilian life," he said, shifting in his seat. "It's been tough."

"If there is anything you need or if you wish to talk, I hear Pastor Howell is excellent in giving counsel and a hand." Mrs. Hammond gave a side glance towards her husband. "Although not everyone will admit when they need help."

Mr. Hammond's head jerked up, and he glared at Mrs. Hammond. "Not everyone wants an old, meddling man in their business."

"Well, if it can help, I don't see a problem talking with him," Mrs. Hammond countered, slamming the coffee pot on the table and placing her hand on her hip.

"What makes Pastor Howell the expert? When did he serve in the military? What atrocities has he seen or had to live through to make it possible for him to relate? You're ignorant if you think that man has sage wisdom to offer anyone at this table," Mr. Hammond spat out in anger.

"Don't talk about him like that, Luke. You can

be angry all you want, but you don't have to be disrespectful to a man you used to call a friend."

"He was never my friend, just the childhood sweetheart of my wife. Maybe your feelings about George Howell are clouding your judgment. I haven't forgotten the rumors of how sweet you were on him while in school back before you met and married me. Maybe you decided to rekindle that relationship while I was away fighting in this wretched war."

Mrs. Hammond turned bright red as she shook her head in humiliation. "Stop it, Luke, stop it, right now. I can't believe you would accuse me of such a baseless, despicable lie. You're embarrassing me."

"I'm embarrassing you? You invited people into my house and forced me to spend time with them to show me the error of my ways." Grabbing the vase from the table, Mr. Hammond threw it across the room. It landed on the wall and shattered into pieces.

Hope came rushing towards them as Mrs. Hammond burst into tears. Everyone was silent as Faith stood up and moved behind her chair to pick up the glass shards from the ground.

After Mrs. Hammond gathered her composure,

she instructed, "Leave it, Faith. I'll take care of it later."

"We should go now," Nathan said, standing from the table and wanting to escape the uncomfortable situation.

"Let me save you the trouble and I'll go first." Mr. Hammond jumped from the table, picked up his crutch, and headed out of the room. A few minutes later, a door slammed from the upstairs part of the house.

Mrs. Hammond shook her head in aversion, dabbing at the tears on her cheek with a handkerchief she had pulled from the pocket of her apron. "I'm so sorry both of you had to witness that horrible display."

"It's not your fault, Mrs. Hammond. You're doing the best you can," Faith responded.

"Thank you for coming over tonight but we need to clean up now. I have an early morning," Mrs. Hammond excused.

Nathan took Faith's hand and moved towards the door. Before leaving, Faith stopped and turned around to face the Hammond women. "Can we pray with you before we go?" Faith inquired.

Mother and daughter looked at each other, then nodded. "We would like that," Hope stated.

Faith and Nathan stepped forward and took their hands, the four of them forming a circle as Faith prayed. "Dear Lord, right now we come to You and ask for Your presence in this situation. We know You love each of us through the good times and the bad, so we pray Mr. Hammond feels Your love even in these dark times. We know You work all things together for our good. In Jesus' name, we pray, Amen."

After leaving the Hammond home, Nathan looked at Faith with admiration. "You were wonderful with them. I can't believe how lucky I am to have a woman with such strong faith."

"I guess my mother knew what she was doing when she gave me my name," Faith teased.

"You definitely live up to your name," Nathan agreed. "I wish I had a measure of the faith you do right now. I just can't seem to find a way back to how I used to be."

"You don't have to do it alone, Nathan. I'm here for you, as is the whole family, but most importantly, God is here for you, too. You just need to find a way to trust all of us again."

As they walked to the Abernathy farm, Nathan was deep in thought. Why was he behaving the way he was? He was exactly where he wanted to be. His desire to return to Faith and her family was what kept him going while he had been a prisoner. He had relied so heavily on his faith during that time, but since being back in Myrtle Grove, it was like he was disconnected from everything, including God.

Nathan wasn't sure how, but he needed to find a way to fix it. The last thing he wanted was to end up like Luke Hammond. He had seen a lot of awful things in his day, but never from a soldier directed at his family. It made him positive of one thing—he would do whatever it took to keep it from happening to him.

CHAPTER 13

Faith was tilling the family's garden when Hope arrived at the house so they could walk together to the church for the monthly recipe-swap meeting.

"Do you need help?" Hope inquired, leaning over the wooden fence.

Faith looked at her friend's clean attire with a raised eyebrow. She didn't want to assign any work which would dirty her outfit. "Sure; if you don't mind, follow behind with the watering can while I finish weeding this last row."

Hope picked up the nearby metal can and followed Faith's instructions. "I wanted to apologize again for my father's behavior the other day. If I had known he'd act out the way he did, I never would've invited you to come over."

"It isn't your fault. You didn't know that was going to happen. Besides, you can't control what other people do."

"How are things going between you and Nathan?" Hope inquired. "Have you decided on a date for the wedding yet?"

"I'm not sure when that's going to happen. Nathan seems to be barely keeping his head above water since he's returned. I will say, though yesterday was difficult for your family, it may have made Nathan realize he needs help. While we're at the swap meeting tonight, he's planning to meet with Pastor Howell."

"Well, if my father's outburst helped Nathan see what he doesn't want to be, something good came from it," Hope said, placing the watering can down after finishing the final row.

"I wish it hadn't been at the expense of you and your mother though," Faith added, placing the hoe against the fence.

"We'll manage. We have for nearly a year now," Hope pointed out with a determined smile.

"What are you doing here, Hope?" Faith heard her brother ask from behind them.

Both women spun around to find Davis staring at them. To be more accurate, his eyes were fixed on Hope as if he didn't care who else was around them.

"I came to walk with your sister to church for the recipe-swap meeting," Hope explained.

"It's good to see you again," Davis said, giving her an appreciative look.

"Thank you, Davis. I'm happy to see you too."

"Are you ladies excited about getting new recipes to try out?"

Both of the women nodded as Hope stated, "I've been looking forward to it all week."

"It should be an interesting night, to say the least," Faith added, as she thought about how the event had changed.

In the beginning, it had been a few women who met up and traded recipes they received in pamphlets about the war. In typical Myrtle Grove tradition, however, something which started out so simple morphed into an elaborate event.

There were three categories now: substitutes, meatless, and sugarless. Each woman could bring one recipe per category. Faith had created her own version of cornbread stuffing, a meatless casserole, and the molasses apple pie. She had made each one several times, and had settled on family-approved versions. The baked dish had been quick for Faith to figure out, but the other two dishes proved more difficult. She had always been a better baker than cook, which caused her to look forward to new savory recipes she would receive at the event.

Davis shrugged. "I can walk with you over to the church. I need to get a few items from the general store anyway."

Faith was skeptical of Davis' motives. Was he making an excuse to go with them? She hadn't heard mother or father say they needed him to get anything. She suspected he desired to spend more time with Hope.

"How kind of you to offer, Davis. We would love that, wouldn't we, Faith?"

She could see from her friend's expression and posture, she wanted Faith to agree. Who was she to argue? "I think it would be nice."

Just at that moment, Nathan arrived at the garden. His hands were shoved in his pocket as he asked, "Are you ladies ready to go?"

"Almost. Let me get out of this grimy outfit and change into a clean dress," Faith explained as she gestured to her work clothes. "I'll grab our supplies, Hope, after I finish getting ready."

After a few minutes passed, Faith appeared in her fresh, blue, day dress, carrying her mother's tapestry bag.

"Do we need to wait on Mother and Ida?" Davis inquired.

"No, they told me they will catch up with us later. They're waiting on Grandmother to get ready," Faith explained.

The four of them set off for the church and fell into pairs with Nathan and Faith in front. Davis and Hope walked behind them. Conversation passed easily between the couples. Faith could hear Hope laughing at the stories Davis told her, some of them not even funny enough to merit a laugh. Hope must be smitten with her brother to react in such a way. Why hadn't Faith noticed the connection between them before? It was so obvious now, she wondered how long it had been going on. Later she would have to ask Hope to fill her in on the details of how and when it had started.

They arrived at the church and Nathan gave Faith a hug. "Enjoy your time. I look forward to sampling your new recipes. I'll pick you up after it ends." After releasing her, Nathan headed towards the back of the church to the pastor's office.

Faith wondered what her brother planned to do.

His focus remained on Hope as he stated, "I suppose I need to be heading over to the general store. Would you like me to come back after your meeting is over to walk you home?"

Hope nodded with a smile. "That would be lovely."

As the women entered the church, the middle of the room was thick with the townswomen preparing for the swap. There was noise from the different women talking to one another. The pews lined the back wall and square tables sat in the center in two lines facing each other. The other women claimed the majority of the tables, but there was one empty one at the end of the far row.

Faith and Hope made their way over to the vacant spot. Faith opened the tapestry bag with their table decorations and placed the basic light pink tablecloth across their table. Next, she put a small bouquet of wildflowers in the middle of their table.

As Faith looked around the room, she noticed several other tables were covered with more decorations than she had brought. Several had tablecloths in various rich colors, coordinating table runners if they had them, and multiple flower arrangements and candles. The women seemed to have used what little fine items they had left to decorate their tables.

Her eyes fell to her own spot, and she felt a drop in her stomach. She should have put more thought into it, but she had been preoccupied with Nathan's return. It didn't help that there wasn't much left in their home to use. Faith had decided against asking Hope, as she was dealing with a lot with her family, not to mention they had even less than the Abernathys. She hoped her friend wouldn't be upset with what she had brought.

"I didn't bring adequate embellishments to keep up with everyone else," Faith confessed.

Hope rolled her eyes. "Don't be upset with yourself over it. There was no way we could compete with Sarah, Susan and Wendy anyway." Hope leaned towards Faith and added, "Besides, all of this seems so frivolous with all our men fighting in the war. Don't get caught up in their competitive nonsense."

Faith nodded, then looked across at the tables of the women Hope named. Sure enough, their tables were the most extravagant.

As all the ladies finished the final touches to their tables and added their stacks of recipes, Virginia Howell, the pastor's wife, made her way to the center of the room. As she raised her hand in the air, everyone quieted down for her to speak in her friendly Southern accent.

"Welcome ladies. It's so wonderful to see all of you. I'm excited to receive delicious, new recipes." Mrs. Howell gave a pointed stare at a few tables. "I see the table decorating has become exceptional this month. I'd like to remind all of you, we're doing this to support our men who are fighting against the tyranny of the north. God would want us to take part with a spirit of camaraderie. Please keep that in mind."

There were a few murmurs as several of the women crossed their arms and sullen expressions took possession of their faces. Guilty consciences perhaps?

Mrs. Howell replaced her admonishing look with a bright smile. "Let's get this evening under way. Enjoy the samples from last month's recipes on the refreshment table and happy swapping."

After Faith and Hope placed their recipes at their spot, they made their way from table to table, picking up a set of recipes from each of the other women. Only a few minutes had passed when

Faith heard raised voices next to her. She turned her attention toward the commotion.

"I can't believe you did this, Sarah. I told you in confidence I was swapping a meatless stew recipe," Wendy accused, as she shook a recipe card in her friend's face.

"You think just because you brought a stew recipe, Wendy, no one else can make something similar?" With an irritated shrug, Sarah stated, "I wanted to make a soup for the upcoming change in seasons, so I did."

The argument was escalating into a full-blown fight as Wendy placed her hands on her hips. "You may call it a soup but it's the exact recipe I had you sample earlier this week for my stew." Sarah tried to move away, but Wendy reached out and grabbed her by the arm. "I had plans to enter it in the county fair once the war is over. You know because I told you."

Sarah pulled away and stated, "I don't remember you saying that."

With a narrowed glare, Wendy shouted, "Don't act forgetful. That might work with your husband, but it won't with me. You stole my recipe because you knew how good it had turned out."

"Why not let everyone else decide which one is

better? They can try both recipes and then we'll know who created the best one." Moving back to her table, Sarah sat down in the chair behind it. "I'm sorry you're upset, but I'll swap whatever recipe I want. There is nothing you can do about it."

Apparently, Wendy thought there was something she could do as she grabbed up Sarah's pile of recipes and started ripping them apart. Sarah jumped to her feet and reached across the table to pull them from her grasp. The women were pulling back and forth with the stack of recipes between them.

"Ladies, that is enough!" Mrs. Howell commanded with authority. "You will not behave like this in the house of the Lord." Stepping between them, she reached out and took the recipes from the women. With a chiding whisper, she stated, "You both should be ashamed of yourselves behaving like this."

The rebuke worked. Both women stepped back and their heads sagged towards the floor.

Mrs. Howell addressed the group. "The only way to fix the problem is to remove both recipes from this month's swap. I want to recommend, as we go forward, if you share your intentions with anyone before the swap, do so at your own risk."

After the fight ended, the room settled down into a normal rhythm and several people commented on Faith's recipes, saying they couldn't wait to try them out. The one she looked forward to trying most was for substituting okra seeds for coffee beans. If she carefully parched them and then used them to make coffee in the usual way, it would replicate coffee in color as well as have a very pleasant taste, according to Bonnie, who had brought the recipe.

Faith was grateful for all the new dishes she could cook for Nathan and her family over the next month, as well as some time where she didn't have to think about the war or what it was doing to her life.

CHAPTER 14

Pastor Howell greeted Nathan with a grin as he reached out and patted Nathan on the back. "Come in, come in."

Though the office was small, it had room for a bookshelf, two chairs and a desk. Nathan followed the pastor over to the chairs where the elderly man gestured for Nathan to sit down next to him.

"Glad to see you kept your appointment with me. I half expected you to cancel the way you reacted on Sunday to my invitation."

"I considered it, but something occurred to cause me to realize I need to work through what transpired while I was in the military."

"You mean, while you were a prisoner," Pastor Howell clarified.

Nathan stiffened and forced himself not to react. He needed to confront what happened to move past it, but every time he thought about his experience in the Union prison, he felt like he was sinking into an endless crater of darkness.

When Nathan didn't respond, Pastor Howell inquired, "What caused you to change your mind about coming here today?"

Nathan crossed his arms against his chest. "We had dinner over at the Hammonds' home Sunday night."

Pastor Howell rubbed his brown beard, then shook his head. "Let me guess, Luke Hammond wasn't exactly hospitable."

"To say the least. It made me realize I don't want to end up like that. I want to marry Faith and start our future together."

"Which means, you need to make peace with your past," Pastor Howell stated plainly. "I'm guessing, it's compounded by your previous time in the military."

As Nathan rolled his shoulders, he averted his eyes. "Yes, I have immense guilt over what I did the first time I served in the military, but that has nothing to do with what I'm going through now."

"Doesn't it? Guilt clouds our ability to accept

the truth. God has forgiven all of our trespasses, yet we still hold on to our wrongdoings. It's hard to accept sometimes, but we don't have to punish ourselves over the poor choices we have made. God wants to free us from our pain and guilt."

Nathan continued to stare at the ground in front of him. He didn't have the courage to look Pastor Howell in his eyes. "Easy to say if you're dealing with minor mistakes like stealing an apple or calling someone a name, but the things I've done, Pastor Howell, are unforgivable. I've spent the last couple of years trying to live a good life to make up for what I did while trying not to think about it. Just when I thought I might be able to put it behind me, I was taken because of it. What I went through while they held me captive, it made me live it all over again."

Pastor Howell reached out and patted Nathan's arm. "That's just it, Nathan, you don't need to make up for it. God has already paid the wages for it."

"Then why won't the guilt go away?"

"Because you haven't forgiven yourself. Until you do, it never will."

This time, Nathan's head popped up and his

eyes met Pastor Howell's kind, blue gaze. Nathan could see the compassion the older man reflected.

With an understanding look, Pastor Howell posed a question. "Is it possible, part of you believes you deserved what happened to you while you were imprisoned?"

The thought had never occurred to Nathan. Was it conceivable his guilt caused him to feel like he hadn't deserved to have God intervene and save him? If that was the case, it would explain why the guilt wouldn't go away.

"Pastor Howell, it's possible you're right. I haven't made peace with my past, which means I can't move forward with my future. Do you mind praying with me to help me find a way?"

"I'm glad you understand the need for prayer, Nathan. We should continue to meet. This is a safe place for you to talk, and anything you say stays just between the two of us."

Nathan was grateful he had someone he could confide in about all he had gone through. He needed to trust the Lord with his whole heart, even the parts he had kept buried deep inside.

CHAPTER 15

Sudden shouting from the church entrance echoed through the room. All the women looked to see what was happening.

"You can't keep me out, Virginia. I know my daughter is in there and I demand you let me go find her."

Oh-no, it was Mr. Hammond; poor Hope. How was she going to handle this? He sounded drunk and belligerent.

Faith watched in horror as Mr. Hammond hobbled past Mrs. Howell in a huff, and over to Faith and Hope's table. His words slurred as he spoke. "There you are, Hope. I thought I made it clear I didn't want you involved in any more of these events. This war has already taken enough from us and our family isn't giving one more ounce for it. You need to follow me out of here this instant," Mr. Hammond commanded.

Hope turned bright red. "Father, you're embarrassing me."

"I don't care if I'm embarrassing you," Mr. Hammond's eyes narrowed as he spat out. "You defied my orders and I'll not have it."

"You're mistaken, Father. You never told me not to come," Hope insisted.

"Don't you dare contradict me! I know what I said." He moved around the table and grabbed Hope by the wrist, causing her to flinch and let out a small cry.

Faith's eyes grew round with fear. Unnoticed, she moved away to go get Nathan from the church office. The townswomen needed a man to deal with Mr. Hammond. As she slipped out of the door of the church, she rushed down the stairs. Before she could turn the corner towards the back though, she heard Davis inquire, "What are you doing out here? Is everything all right?"

With a shake of her head, Faith stated, "No, everything is far from all right. I was going to get Nathan because Mr. Hammond is inside and causing a scene with Hope."

"How bad is it?"

"He's drunk and doesn't realize he's hurting her."

Davis charged past Faith towards the church entrance. As Faith followed behind her brother, she pressed, "What are you going to do?"

"I can take care of it."

"I realize you care about Hope, but should you get involved?"

Faith was worried her brother might get hurt, or worse, hurt Mr. Hammond. No good would come from either act happening.

"Someone has to, and I'm as good as anyone. Besides, I'm not about to let anything happen to Hope." His protectiveness over her friend proved to Faith she had assumed right about what was going on between her brother and best friend. Davis certainly had feelings for Hope.

As they entered the church, Mr. Hammond still had Hope by the wrist, and was yelling at her about her behavior. Hope's eyes were downcast, and she looked like she wanted to melt away on the spot.

Davis walked up to them and gently placed his hand on the elderly man's shoulder. "Mr. Hammond, this event is for the women in town. Why don't I take you home?"

Mr. Hammond let go of Hope and turned his attention to Davis. "I'm not sure how any of this is your business."

"I never said it was, but your shouting is disrupting the event. It's best if you leave."

With an angry shrug, Mr. Hammond snapped, "I'll be glad to leave just as soon as my obstinate daughter agrees to leave with me. She shouldn't have come to this ridiculous gathering in the first place. She's going home with me, now!" Mr. Hammond grabbed Hope's wrist a second time and attempted to pull her towards the door. He stumbled slightly, barely catching himself before he fell.

Hope's eyes grew round with fear, causing Davis to interject. "Can't you see you're upsetting your daughter?"

"I don't care if she's upset. It's her own fault for coming here."

Davis reached out and removed Mr. Hammond's hand from his daughter. "She shouldn't go with you in your current condition. I can bring her home after the swap concludes."

"How dare you, boy! I can tell you're trying to impress my girl. It's obvious you're sweet on her, but let me remind you, you'll need my blessing to pursue her. You lost any chance of that tonight."

"You have no inkling of my motives, Mr. Hammond. I simply want to keep Hope safe."

"Are you implying she isn't safe with me? I'm her father for goodness' sake!" Mr. Hammond bellowed.

"Then act like it," Davis asserted with audible irritation.

Mr. Hammond dropped Hope's wrist and looked at her. "Do I make you feel unsafe?"

"I wish it weren't true, but yes, Father, you make me feel unsafe when you're like this."

A momentary expression of hurt flashed across Mr. Hammond's face before he shook his head and stumbled towards the exit, mumbling under his breath about ungratefulness.

Once he left the premise, Faith turned to face her friend. With concern, she rushed towards Hope and lifted her wrist to inspect it. "Are you harmed?"

"I'm fine," Hope pulled her wrist free and hid it behind her back. "Humiliated but fine."

"Don't be. No one here blames you for your father's actions," Davis insisted.

"I shouldn't have come. I should've known it would upset him," Hope whispered, with a dejected look on her face.

"You can't live your life to appease him," Faith

stated with frustration. "No matter what you do, it won't be enough until he deals with what happened to him."

As she said the words, Faith realized she was talking as much about Nathan as she was Mr. Hammond. Nathan needed to deal with happened to him too, but he couldn't seem to find a way to do it. Silently, Faith sent up a prayer for both men.

Hope looked around the room as she pressed her lips together. Giving Faith a tearful look, she whispered, "I don't want to be here anymore. Everyone is watching me."

"Why don't we go over to the café. I'll get us a cup of coffee and dessert," Davis offered.

"Thank you," Hope whispered as she extended her hand to him, which he took and placed on his arm. Once they left the room, Faith moved back over to the table and sat down. She hadn't even realized it, but her own body had nearly given out from fright.

A few minutes later, Faith's mother, sister, and grandmother arrived and joined her at her table. She hugged them, saying, "I'm so glad you are all here. Tonight has been dreadful."

"What happened?" Her mother asked with concern.

Faith filled them in on what transpired before heading over to the refreshment table to grab her family some treats. She grabbed a small plate and picked up a few samples of flourless pastries, meatless appetizers and molasses cookies. She also poured herself a cup of sugarless lemonade.

Before she headed back to the table, Faith nibbled on one of the cookies. As usual, it tasted delicious. The women in Myrtle Grove sure knew how to cook and bake, even without the help of commonly used ingredients.

As she looked around the room, she realized how lucky she was to be a part of a close-knit community. Faith enjoyed spending time with the other women from her town and there was always something for which she could volunteer or get involved. It helped keep her mind off the problems in her life, even if it was only a temporary reprieve.

"Why have you been standing here by yourself for so long?" Bonnie pried as she ambled up to Faith.

"I was just taking a break."

"Oh, dear, are you having a hard time because of all that is going on with you and Nathan?"

Faith's head jerked towards Bonnie as her eyes

narrowed in annoyance. "What are you talking about?"

"It's obvious Nathan hasn't been the same since he returned home," she leaned towards Faith and whispered, "after those degenerate Union mercenaries took him captive."

Faith's defenses took over, still trying to protect Nathan from people's scrutiny. She placed her plate and cup on the corner of a table as she asked, "How did you hear about that?"

Bonnie reached out and patted Faith on the arm. "Everyone knows, dear. It's no secret. I want you to know I'm here for you; no matter how all of this turns out."

Faith's brows furrowed together in confusion. "How what turns out? I'm not sure what you're talking about."

"Why, your wedding, of course. With all Nathan has been through, he's a different man now. You two might not find your way through this, and if that happens, you'll have to let him go. You'll need your friends and family around you to help you through it."

Yanking her arm away from Bonnie, Faith stated in anger, "Never! That will never happen. I'll never give up on Nathan or what we have together."

With a sympathetic expression, Bonnie soothed, "Oh, dear, you're still so young. You think love can conquer all, but you haven't been around long enough to realize that just isn't true."

With conviction, Faith insisted, "You're right, love may not conquer all, but God can. He's what holds us together. He'll get us through this difficult season just like he has everything else."

Faith rushed past Bonnie, fighting back the tears that threatened to fall at any moment. She didn't stop at her table, but blew right past her family, knowing that at any moment she would be a heaving sob.

Once outside, Faith headed over to the oak tree in the corner of the property. Her attention focused on their initials and her finger traced the letters once more.

F.A.

+

N.M.

Concentrating on it helped her remain calm, and kept the tears from falling. When they had put them there before he left, Faith thought it meant they would be together forever. Had she been foolish to believe so blindly? Nathan was still distant. She wasn't sure if they could ever bridge the gap between them.

Faith felt an arm wrap around her waist and felt breath against her neck, just before Nathan announced, "It seems we had the same idea. I was planning to come and wait here by the oak tree for you, but you beat me to it." Nathan pulled her around to face him. "Is the meeting over?"

"Almost; I had to step out and take a break. It's been a long night."

Nathan released Faith from his hold and moved to lean against the tree next to her. "Did something happen?"

"Mr. Hammond came here and fought with Hope."

Nathan's eyebrows drew up in surprise. "Do I need to do something about it?"

"No, Davis took care of it, and I thought everything would calm down. Then something else happened."

"You weren't kidding it was an eventful night. What occurred next?"

"Bonnie." Faith didn't need to say anything

more. Everyone in town knew Bonnie could make just about anyone desire a break.

"I'm sorry you had to deal with her this evening. Did she do something specific this time, or just the typical bothersome behavior?"

"She thinks we won't get married."

His eyes grew wide with disbelief as he slumped against the tree in anger. "What would give her that impression?"

Faith let out a heavy sigh as she shook her head. "Nathan, I've been trying to protect you from the truth, but you should know, everyone sees how you've been conducting yourself since you've returned."

"What does that mean?"

"You came home, but you're not here," she stated bluntly. "What happened to you was so damaging, no one thinks we're going to make it to the altar because of it."

Faith braced herself for Nathan to argue the point. He wasn't one to accept defeat. Instead he stated, "It's true."

Her heart dropped to her stomach as her body started to quiver. "It's really over then. You don't want to be with me anymore," Faith squeaked out in despair.

Nathan pushed off the tree and reached out to grab her. He pulled her towards him, holding her in his embrace. "No, that's not what I mean. I will never leave you, Faith. I'm talking about the second part. You're right about me not being here. I haven't been because I was still stuck in that prison. I might have escaped physically, but the rest of me is still trapped in a cage."

It was the first time he had admitted there was a problem out loud. His confession took her by surprise; she could hardly believe it.

"All of that will change now. I realized I can't handle this on my own. I require support, which is why I agreed to continue meeting with Pastor Howell twice a week to talk about what took place. We prayed tonight, and I felt a small piece of my burden lift away. I know God can help me."

Faith leaned back and gazed up into Nathan's eyes. A small smile formed on her face as she whispered, "I'm so glad to hear that Nathan. All I want is for you to be okay."

"There is one more thing I need for that to happen."

"And what might that be?" Faith implored.

"You. I need you by my side, always and forever." He placed his hand under her chin and tilted her head up as his lips descended to meet her own.

It was the first time he had kissed her with passion since returning home from the war. The intensity of the kiss took her breath away. She felt her knees go weak as his arms wrapped around her waist. Faith melted into his loving embrace as the distance between them faded away.

CHAPTER 16

Two weeks passed as Nathan and Faith mended their relationship. Nathan returned to his old routine from before he left for the war. He labored on the plantation with Faith's father and brothers during the first part of the day, and worked on finishing their home in the late afternoons.

After nailing the final wall into place, Nathan looked at his accomplishment with pride. It felt good to work with his hands and to see his efforts manifest a home for his future family. He imagined their little children running around in the yard while he and Faith watched from the porch.

The thought spurred the next project on his list. He still needed to stucco the house and then build the porch. Once he finished the two tasks, Faith could paint the inside and their home would be ready just in time for their wedding in early October.

Faith's father came up and patted Nathan on the back. "It's looking good. I envision a happy couple living in this place and the many, many, grandchildren you'll make me."

Nathan's head lurched to the side as his eyes grew round with worry. "How many children are you planning on us having?"

"At least as many as Tabitha and I have," he stated with a serious expression. A few seconds passed before he chuckled. "I'm just kidding. You two need to decide how many children you want. Although, I know Faith has said on more than one occasion she wants three at minimum."

Three children? Nathan could handle three children, couldn't he? Faith was a determined woman and did an expert job of convincing Nathan that what she wanted was what he desired. He saw a future with little hands pulling on his pant legs with chocolate-covered faces smiling up at him.

"I'll guarantee you one thing; I plan to make your daughter happy. Besides, I love kids, so I guess I can assure you we'll do our best to make you a grandfather multiple times."

"Glad we agree. I hear being a grandfather is one of the greatest joys this world has to offer. I find it hard to believe any experience touches the joys of being a father, but I hope I'm proven wrong."

Laughter filled the afternoon air as the rest of the Abernathy family arrived. Tabitha was holding a picnic basket while Ida carried two blankets. Faith's grandparents were walking beside them as Jack and Nancy were running around chasing each other. Davis and Faith brought up the rear.

"We thought everyone deserved time to enjoy the wonderful autumn weather as a reward for being diligent in their work," Thomas stated as the family came to join them.

"You're doing an impressive job, Nathan," Mortimer declared as he looked at the freshly plastered house.

"Thank you. I hope your granddaughter thinks so."

Faith placed her hand on Nathan's arm. "I do. I can't wait until we get married and move into it."

"It will be ready for you to paint by the end of the week."

"I suppose that means I need to go into town and pick out colors. Do you mind taking me in tomorrow?"

"I'll be happy to take you," Nathan agreed with a grin. Taking her hands in his own, he asked, "Where have you decided we will picnic?"

"We were thinking in the meadow behind the house."

"Okay, lead the way," Nathan said, placing her hand in the crook of his arm.

As the group walked over to the grassland, the meadow was fragrant from the blooming wildflowers which laced the field in an array of colors. The family weaved through the meadow following a small path, and towards the center found a spot to lay their blankets.

Nancy and Jack continued to play in the meadow as the women took out the food and napkins from the picnic basket. The men sat on the edge of the blanket and watched as the spread of appealing cuisine appeared; potted cheese and crackers, chicken sandwiches, fruit salad and peach cake. The women unwrapped and placed the food on the blankets. There also were several containers of sun-tea along with wooden cups.

"Nancy and Jack, come over here and sit down," Tabitha called to her children. Obediently, they joined the rest of the family on the blanket.

"Let us say grace before we eat." Everyone

bowed their heads before Thomas prayed. "Dear Lord, thank You for this wonderful day You have given us. We pray for safety for the soldiers still fighting in the war, and for us to continue to do our part here. We pray for Your sustained blessing on our family. We thank You for bringing Nathan home to us. In the Lord's name, Amen."

As soon as Faith handed Nathan his food, he dove into the delectable fare. He'd worked up a large appetite working on finishing the house. His taste buds exploded with flavor as he took each bite.

The picnic passed with ease as they talked about the day, the plantation, and church. After they finished, Nathan stretched out as he declared, "The meal was delicious. You ladies did a wonderful job of preparing this picnic."

"Thank you, Nathan," the women's voices rang out in unison. They looked at each other in shock for several seconds before everyone laughed.

Nathan stood up and reached out to take Faith's hand as he requested, "Would you care to go for a stroll?"

Before Faith could respond, Nancy whined, "I thought you were going to play tag with me, Nathan?"

"How about when I get back? I promise I'll play with you for a few minutes before we go home."

The pout instantly turned into a giant grin. "Yippee, I can't wait!"

"Can I play too?" Jack chimed in.

"Of course; it's more fun with extra people. Maybe we can talk the whole family into playing."

"My days of playing tag are far behind me," Mortimer brusquely stated.

"Okay, so maybe just the Abernathy children," Nathan amended, realizing that none of the senior members would find the act appealing.

"Don't count me out just because my husband is being a stick in the mud," Pearl jested.

Everyone began to laugh and the dulcet sound echoed through the meadow. Nathan patted Nancy on the head and then drew Faith up beside him, folding her hand into his own as they started down the path. Thomas called out from behind them, "Don't wander too far."

Nathan knew Thomas wasn't worried for their safety but more for his daughter's virtue. Even though they were getting married soon, her father still didn't allow them to spend any length of time alone together. Nathan didn't mind. He would be just as protective with his own future daughters.

Faith broke the silence. "How have your meetings with Pastor Howell been going?"

"Beneficial. I understand why I behaved the way I did, and through Pastor Howell's guidance, I've given my guilt and past over to God. I'm free for the first time in my life."

Faith squeezed Nathan's hand in excitement. "I'm pleased to hear it, Nathan. You deserve to be happy."

"No one deserves to be happy, but I hope God will bless our life together, and give us what we need."

Faith nodded. "You're right; God gives us what we need, not always what we want. Your time with Pastor Howell has given you insight."

Nathan stopped and turned to face Faith. "I've been wanting to share something with you for a while now. Something I haven't told anyone else."

A worried look crossed her face. "What is it?"

"Something profound happened to me when I escaped Union captivity. I told you it wasn't the military who found me."

Her body relaxed as the concern melted from her face. "Yes, I remember. You never explained in detail what happened, and I didn't want to press you."

Nathan wanted to blurt it out, but something was keeping him from saying the words out loud. Part of him worried Faith wouldn't believe what he told her. Another part of him worried she might think him crazy. If someone told him what he was about to tell her, he would.

She placed her hand on the side of his arm as she whispered, "You know you can tell me anything."

As he stared into her forest green eyes, he felt confident he could finally tell her what happened. He took a deep breath, then revealed the truth of how he escaped. "God sent an angel to rescue me. The angel guided me out of the place where they were keeping me and lead me to where Peter was waiting."

Faith was silent for several moments before she spoke, as if contemplating the magnitude of what he just confessed. Every moment she remained silent, he wondered if she were going to think he had lost his mind. He wouldn't blame her. He could hardly believe it himself, and it had happened to him.

Finally, after what seemed like a lifetime, Faith finally spoke. "God went to great lengths not only to save you but to give you such a powerful experience.

When you're ready, God will open the door for you to use it for His glory."

Nathan's heart swelled at the love and acceptance Faith constantly offered him. "You don't know how glad I am to finally tell you that and have you react in such a positive way. God knows I need you, Faith, and I'm so glad He brought you into my life. Thank you for not giving up on me."

"I hope by now you know I never will. You're my life. I'll always stand by you no matter what," Faith vowed.

Nathan leaned down and pressed his lips against Faith's. It was gentle at first, manifested from gratitude, but as he pulled her close and enfolded her in his embrace, the kiss deepened as the passion surfaced between them. Faith wrapped her arms around Nathan's neck as the kiss continued. He felt the rapid beating of her heart as her body leaned against his own. His body wanted him to allow the kiss to continue but his head told him it was time to stop.

Nathan forced himself to end the kiss. "We should make our way back. We will have plenty of time for this in two weeks."

Faith averted her eyes as she blushed. "Agreed.

I'm sure my parents are expecting our arrival at any moment."

With a chuckle, he joked, "I want to get you back before your dad has my hide."

Nathan grabbed Faith's hand for the return trip to the picnic area. As he looked out over the meadow, he saw their future home in the distance with the sun setting behind it. The sky was lit with golden hues of pink, lavender, and burnt orange. The sunset was magnificent, but as Nathan turned to look at Faith, he realized nothing could be more breathtaking than the woman he was going to marry.

CHAPTER 17

Myrtle Grove Church was bustling with commotion when Faith walked inside with her family and Nathan. Faith noticed the surrounding faces appeared troubled. Several of the women's eyes were red and puffy, testaments to the fact they had been crying.

"What's going on?" Faith inclined her head towards her mother.

"I'm uncertain, but I want to find out. I know just who can help fill us in." Faith's mother made her way over to Bonnie, Joanna, Sarah, and Wendy who were standing together in a hushed huddle. Faith followed her mother, wanting to find out for herself what had the church parishioners upset.

"Good morning, ladies." Faith's mother greeted

the other women as she took her place amongst their circle.

Bonnie shared the unfortunate news. "There's an outbreak of Influenza in Chapmin. Several people came down with the sickness, and Mrs. Potter passed away yesterday morning."

Sarah shook her head. "She had six children. What are they going to do without their mother?"

"I don't know. The delivery man from Chapmin told me Mr. Potter was beside himself, the poor man," Wendy stated.

"We should do something for the family; perhaps take over food, and wash laundry for them," Tabitha suggested.

"Even though Lilly, their oldest, is thirteen, it will be too much for her to handle on her own," added Joanna in agreement.

"Should we wait to make sure everyone is healthy before going?" Bonnie questioned with concern.

Anxious expressions crossed the other women's faces before Tabitha scolded, "What would Jesus have us do? He'd want us to help the Potter family now and not worry about such things. He'll keep us safe while we're doing His work."

The women nodded as Pastor Howell asked for everyone to sit for the service.

As Faith took her seat in her family's pew, she wondered if the sickness would make its way to Myrtle Grove. Even though she knew she shouldn't fear it happening, it was hard to give her trepidation to God with the palpable fear in the room.

Pastor Howell must have sensed the mood because he started the service with a prayer.

"Dear Lord, we come together as a church and ask for You to please be with our brothers and sisters in Chapmin. Pour mercy on the families affected by the sickness and heal those who are still battling with it. Keep our town safe and free from the illness. We ask You to stop it from spreading. In Jesus' name, Amen."

The tension evaporated, allowing the service to go ahead without distress.

Pastor Howell gave a message about making peace with the past and giving guilt over to God. Towards the end of service, he offered a time for church members to share what God was doing in their lives. Nathan felt prodding from the Lord to share his story.

After several other people went, Nathan stood up

and made his way to the front of the church. "Hello everyone. Please bear with me as I'm uncomfortable doing this. I tend to keep to myself and it's hard for me to open up to people. I returned home from the war a few weeks ago. Adjusting back has been diffi-cult, but all of you, especially the Abernathy family and my fiancée, Faith, have been patient with me. Your support means a great deal. I'm so grateful to be a member of Myrtle Grove Church."

Nathan looked out at all the smiling faces, and felt his nervousness fall away. "Most of you know I was taken captive while I was serving in the war. It's still difficult to talk about what happened while I was in prison, but it's important to share that even though it was the darkest time in my life, God was there with me. He never left my side. His strength and mercy sustained me, and when I thought I had no way out from compromising and giving into their demands, the Lord rescued me."

Murmurs formed around the room before Nathan continued. "When I say He rescued me, I mean He sent an angel to guide me out of the awful place they kept me. I know how it sounds. I was in disbelief at the time, not to mention afterwards when I had time to process what happened, but it's true. God sent a literal angel to rescue me. I was always a skeptic of the supernatural, so it astonished me when it happened."

Several loud gasps erupted from the women in the room. "The reason I'm sharing all of this with you is because I think someone out there needs to know God is always with you. Even when you think you're alone, you're not. God has plans for you; plans to prosper you and not to harm you. Take courage in that. Don't dismiss the possibility God can and will send an angel to help you."

Nathan sat back down and a few more people got up and shared. After service, several people came up and thanked Nathan for sharing.

Faith smiled at Nathan as they headed towards the door. "I'm so proud of you for telling your story today." When they reached the bottom of the stairs, they stopped to finish their conversation. "There is power in sharing what God did for you."

"I know there is. It's why I did it. I felt like God told me there was someone who needed to hear it."

"There was," an unfamiliar voice said from beside them.

Both Nathan and Faith turned towards where the comment manifested. Nathan didn't recognize the young man standing to the side of them.

"Pardon?" Nathan inquired.

"My name is Frank Anderson. I served as a medic with the 12th Infantry Division until they discharged me after I suffered an injury during the first conflict. It felt like God had abandoned me. I didn't understand why he took me out of the military before I could help anyone. I'm visiting here with my college friend, Wyatt Hammond, and when I heard you talk today, I knew the Lord was speaking through you to me. Thank you so much for getting up and sharing," Frank affirmed as he extended his hand to Nathan. "I needed to hear what you had to say."

Nathan took the other man's hand and shook it. "I'm glad my story could help."

Wyatt Hammond walked up next to them with a grin on his face. "Glad to see all of you are having time to talk. Frank and I went to medical school together, and I invited him to join us at church today."

Wyatt was Hope's cousin and the town's new doctor, after their previous one retired. He often spent time with all of them, as the Hammond and Abernathy children had grown up together.

"I think all of us should head over to the café for lunch to celebrate Frank visiting us. I can tell I'll like him way more than you already," Nathan jested.

Wyatt pouted in mock hurt for several seconds before all three of the men and Faith laughed.

Hope came up to the group, with Davis next to her. "What's going on over here?"

"We're making plans to go to the café," Faith informed Hope.

"Sounds like fun. Count us in," Davis stated as Hope nodded in agreement.

The group of six made their way across Main Street to the café where they grabbed a large table towards the back. They enjoyed an afternoon of friendship and laughter, everyone temporarily forgetting the war that raged around them.

CHAPTER 18

The last nail was hammered into the final piece of wood, completing the wraparound porch to the house. Nathan smiled at how successfully it had turned out. He was proud he had finished the home with his own two hands, despite having to take it slow due to his body, which was still healing. It had been a solitary project, and the work therapeutic. Along with his meetings with Pastor Howell, Nathan felt he was putting the past behind him.

Nathan made his way back to the Abernathy plantation. As he saw the house appear on the horizon, he realized it would be one of the last nights he spent in the bunkhouse. Soon, he would marry Faith and start his life with her.

He made his way towards the main house and felt a tinge of weariness shoot up his spine. As Nathan looked around, he expected to see Nancy and Jack playing in the front yard. They were absent along with the normal flurried preparation for the evening meal through the kitchen window. The farm was eerily still. Something was not right.

Nathan scanned the area in all directions. He paused before he entered the house, waiting to hear something to tell him what he would find. The quietness worried him more than the lack of motion. The Abernathy family was anything but quiet. Did that mean there were deserters or thieves trying to take advantage of the Abernathys? There had been rumors that bands of them roamed the countryside looking to take advantage of people.

With quick precision, Nathan swiveled around and sprinted to his room in the bunkhouse. He swung open the door and rushed inside it. At the foot of his twin bed was a trunk with his belongings. He lifted the lid and moved several of the top objects to the side. At the bottom was a small Colt revolver. He pulled it free and checked it. The gun still held the five bullets he had left in it for an emergency.

It felt odd to hold a gun in his hands again.

After his imprisonment in the North, he thought he had left that part of his life behind him. It seemed he still had a job to do with it. As he gripped the gun in his hand, he trotted back towards the main house; his intuition told him to be prepared.

Nathan crouched down and moved along the backside of the house, keeping his body below the window line. He inched up the several steps of the back porch stoop and stopped just outside the door which was ajar, allowing voices to bleed through as Nathan listened. His blood ran cold at the sound of the Northern accents.

"I asked you once already, where is Nathan Maddox?" He recognized Christopher Berns' commanding voice, and knew instantly that his family was in trouble.

Sweat broke out at the edges of Nathan's forehead and neck. Unwanted memories came flooding back of the time he spent under the cruel control of the other man. Nathan forced himself to push the thoughts away and focus on the present. To save his fiancée and her family, he needed to concentrate on what was going on in the other room.

"We told you, we don't know where he is at," Thomas stated firmly.

"Come now, don't play ignorant with me. This

is the home of the woman Nathan planned to marry. It would be the first place he would come to once he was free."

"I'm not arguing the fact we know him; I'm informing you we're unaware of his location at the moment."

"You had better hope for your family's sake he makes a quick return. We only need to keep you alive long enough to force him to come with me. If he figures out what is happening and runs off, your family will pay the price."

"He wouldn't behave that way. He'll never let anything happen to us," Faith insisted resolutely.

Nathan's heart tightened at the sound of Faith's voice. His stomach clenched in anticipation, knowing he needed to live up to the trust she put in him. What was he going to do?

Before he could decide, there was a feminine yelp from the other room. Thomas shouted, "Keep your hands off my daughter!"

Chairs scraped against the wooden floor as the little girls wept and Tabitha begged the man not to harm her family.

A few seconds later, Christopher warned, "May I remind you that my men and I have the power in this situation." With a menacing tone, he added, "Be careful what you say and do next."

The threat must have worked because there was no more commotion. Nathan's grip on the pistol tightened at the thought of Christopher hurting the Abernathys.

"We will sit here and wait until he returns. If any of you warn him, I promise you'll dislike the repercussions."

Christopher had mentioned "his men" which meant he was not alone. If it were just Christopher, the fight would be fair; after all he had trained him and could anticipate his every move. However, if he had soldiers with him, Nathan wouldn't be able to handle multiple assailants at the same time. He needed to separate Christopher from the other men if he stood a chance of saving the Abernathy family.

Covertly, Nathan turned around and crept from the back porch. Once outside again, he grabbed a nearby rock and moved along the edge of the house until he was out of sight. He took a deep breath to steady himself and sent up a silent prayer for protection while tossing the rock at the side of the house.

A few moments later, he heard the shuffling of

feet and saw the screen door swing open. Nathan peeked from around the corner and watched two men stand at the bottom of the steps, looking from side to side.

They didn't wear Union uniforms, but he suspected Christopher was here on an unofficial mission. If that was the case, they would have dressed in civilian clothes to blend in.

"Where do you think the noise came from?" the taller blond man asked the shorter brown-haired fellow.

The shorter man answered, "It was probably just a raccoon or something. Captain Berns gets paranoid on these types of missions." He leaned towards the other man and lowered his voice, "The captain talked headquarters into this assignment, spouting this Maddox was worth the risk for the information he knew. I suspect, however, it's more about revenge for making the captain look like a fool when Maddox escaped his custody."

Christopher was here for revenge. It sounded right. Christopher didn't like being bested, and even if Nathan told him the truth about how he'd gotten away, Christopher wouldn't believe him, anyway.

"We'd better make sure," the taller man stated.

He pointed in the opposite route. "You go around that way and I'll circle in the other direction."

The shorter man shrugged. "If you think it's necessary."

"I'm not getting on the captain's bad side," the other man said with a shudder. "He's killed men for less."

"Fine, but we also don't want to leave the captain too long alone in there, in case that family gets any ideas about fighting back."

The taller man released a blood curdling sadistic laugh. "Did you see their faces after the captain slapped the oldest girl? I don't think we need to worry about that."

"True, but I still don't want to take any chances." The shorter man grumbled, "Let's make this quick."

Heated anger flooded through Nathan. He wanted to march right in the house to punish Christopher for putting his hands on Faith; however, he needed to think about the entire situation. It was imperative he was strategic in how he reacted, or he could risk harming the very people he was trying to protect.

Nathan was grateful that the two soldiers unwittingly divulged the information he needed to know.

It was only three of them in total. It made sense. Christopher couldn't bring a large force this far past the southern border without being detected. Nathan suspected he had used what few contacts and resources he had left in the Confederacy to get this far.

The Union soldiers headed towards their agreed upon routes. Nathan waited a few seconds and then moved after the taller man. He would be harder to take down judging by his size. Nathan wanted to face the bigger man first while he had all his energy still intact.

With swift accuracy, Nathan tucked his gun into the back of his pants and snuck up behind the blond man, reaching up and around his neck. Nathan wasn't short but he could barely reach the man's neck with his arm. However, because he caught him off-guard, Nathan had the advantage. Nathan applied all the pressure he could muster and kept his arm in place across the other man's throat. The soldier struggled but Nathan didn't let go. He held on with all his might until the man swayed and slumped forward.

Nathan lowered the man to the ground and pulled him out of the walkway and into the bushes. The Union soldier would wake up in a few hours with a nasty headache and be turned over to the Confederate military, but at least he'd be alive.

Moving backwards along the house, Nathan headed in the opposite direction to catch the other man before he stumbled upon his comrade.

He saw the brown-haired man meandering along the path. He didn't seem to be looking for anything but following the path out of reluctant obligation. Good. If he wasn't paying attention, he would be easier to take down.

Nathan attacked without warning but he couldn't get a firm grip on the other man's neck. Though he was smaller than the other soldier, he managed to shake free from Nathan's grasp and spin around, swinging at Nathan.

Shocked he'd underestimated the other man, Nathan stumbled back before he could land the punch. This man was more aware than Nathan had given him credit for and seemed to have superior training compared to his last opponent.

Nathan raised his fists up in defense. How could he neutralize the other man before he made enough noise to warn Christopher? His hand-to-hand combat instruction flooded back, and Nathan realized the soldier was expecting a fist fight so he thrusted his left leg out and swiped under the other man's legs. The other man tumbled to the ground as Nathan jumped on top of him. Nathan's hands closed around the soldier's throat as he pressed firmly. He didn't want to kill the other man, but he needed to make sure he couldn't interfere either. Nathan eyed a nearby rock, picked it up and thumped the man over the head just hard enough to knock him out.

Once he was certain the other man was incapacitated, Nathan scrambled off of him. He pushed his back up against the house as his lungs filled with ragged breaths. He closed his eyes and prayed in silence. *Dear Lord, I need your strength right now. Please help me to keep the Abernathy family safe and to end this without bloodshed.*

Rallying the strength to get up, Nathan worked his way towards the back porch. He found himself at the edge of the door listening.

Thomas was in the middle of trying to bargain with Christopher. "Why don't you let my family go? You don't need all of us and I'm more than willing for you to keep me as a hostage."

Nathan knew better than anyone, there was no point. Christopher didn't keep prisoners that didn't have strategic value, and he never let them go alive. He wouldn't hesitate to kill the entire Abernathy family without a second thought once they weren't useful anymore.

"Mr. Abernathy, it's admirable you are trying to save your family, but Nathan's past was bound to catch up with him. If you want someone to blame for what is going to happen to your family, it's him."

"What do you mean by that?" Thomas inquired.

"I mean, your daughter's fiancé is as far from a saint as I am. He's done horrible, despicable things in the name of his country."

"I refuse to listen to you lie about my future son-in-law. Besides, I doubt you have any idea what Nathan has or hasn't done while he served in the military."

"I know first-hand. He trained me and showed me how to be a spy. He's killed people, lots of them, without any remorse. He's used and manipulated women, children, anyone that helped him complete his mission. He's gained people's trust and then betrayed them in ways that were so debased, if it hadn't been in the service of his country, he would have hanged for his actions."

There were audible gasps around the room as

several of the Abernathys said "no" and "not Nathan."

With a flinch, Nathan tried to block out the dismay in their voices. He had worked so hard to keep them from knowing what he had done in his past. Now it was out in the open. What would they think of him? Would they be able to look at him without disgust? Would he be forbidden from marrying Faith, if they were even able to make it out of this alive?

"I don't care what you say," Faith declared fiercely. "Whatever Nathan did in his past can stay there. He has shown himself to be the bravest and kindest man since we have known him. Nothing will change my mind about the man I love."

Just when Nathan thought Faith couldn't prove any more devotion, she astounded him. He would spend the rest of his life trying to be worthy of her love.

CHAPTER 19

"Miss Abernathy, I am tiring of your constant defense of Nathan Maddox."

Faith's eyes grew round and her heart lurched as she stared down the barrel of the Union captain's gun pointed at her. She hated when he talked about Nathan in such a derogatory way and reacted out of protective instinct, not even thinking about her own safety.

"Do I need to teach you another lesson?" he admonished, moving towards her in a menacing manner.

"If you lay a hand on her again, it will be the last thing you ever do."

Faith's eyes darted to the back door as Nathan walked into the room. He held a gun in his hand, raised and leveled at their captor.

"You finally made your way back here, did you, Nathan?" the man taunted, turning his attention to Nathan, who didn't let it affect him.

Nathan continued to stay calm, saying, "I've been here longer than you've been aware."

With a shrug, he stated, "That would explain why my men haven't returned."

"They're not dead, if that concerns you," Nathan explained. "My killing days are behind me, despite what you're trying to make everyone think."

"I don't think so. I think if you had to kill me to save them," Christopher said, gesturing towards Faith and her family, "you would do it without hesitating. The old Nathan is still buried deep inside; you just hid him away very well."

"Think what you want, but you're wrong. I let your men live because I've changed."

"I don't care why you did it. Those men are expendable just as all soldiers are."

What kind of person thought that way? Did Nathan use to think in the same manner? Did part of him still? Faith pushed the troubling thoughts away. She refused to let the Union Captain get to her. She knew who Nathan was, and he was nothing like the soul-less monster standing in front of her.

"What do you want, Christopher?" Nathan probed. "You must have some purpose for coming all this way."

"What I've always wanted, Nathan. For you to return to your rightful place beside me."

"I told you, I'll never go back to that life. My place is here, with Faith and her family."

"And I told you, if you didn't agree to my demands, I would visit Myrtle Grove. Here I am," the captain declared with pride as he reached out and yanked Davis by the arm from his chair. "Should I be keeping my promise and taking this boy as your replacement?"

"I told you back in that prison to never come near the Abernathy family," Nathan growled out as he moved towards his enemy. "Take your hands off him."

The captain placed his hand around the boy's neck as he continued to point the gun at Nathan. "You should know by now you can't tell me what to do."

"I think the reason you're here is because you're jealous of me. I am and will always be, better at everything we're supposed to do as spies. It's why I was in charge and was given the toughest missions. They knew you couldn't get the job done."

"You don't know what you are talking about," Christopher snapped, as his eyes darted around the room, agitation clearly mounting in him.

"Isn't that why you want me?" Nathan questioned as he inched towards the other man. "To prove you can best me, because deep-down you know you'll never measure up to the legacy I created."

What was Nathan doing? He seemed to be baiting the other man, trying to get him to lose control.

"Shut up! Just shut up," Christopher shouted, gesturing wildly with his gun as he narrowed his eyes into angry slits.

Nathan must have been pushing the right buttons because the captain was losing focus and loosening his grip on Davis.

Without warning, Nathan lunged towards Christopher. Davis must have seen it coming because he jumped out of the way just in time to avoid being caught between the two men. Nathan knocked the captain to the ground, and they wrestled on the floor for several seconds.

Faith's father leapt up and rushed towards the

men, grabbing one of the guns which had been knocked free during the fight; however, he couldn't take a shot as the other two men's bodies remained entangled.

They fought on the ground for several seconds with loud grunts and punches echoing through the room. After a few moments, there was a loud blast that filled the room followed by a groan. Christopher collapsed onto Nathan and both men became still.

Faith jumped up, and her hand flew to cover her mouth in alarm. Was Nathan all right? Had the bullet hit him? Was he dead?

Faith's father grabbed the limp body of the Union Captain and pulled it off of Nathan. "Are you okay, Son?"

Nathan blinked several times before responding. "Yes, I'm fine. The weight of him just knocked the wind out of me."

"What happened? How did you stop him?" Davis inquired.

"I'm not sure. From the noise, I assume my gun must have accidentally fired and hit him somewhere."

Davis flipped the other man over and felt for a pulse. "He's alive, but the bullet grazed him on the

side of the head. The impact seems to have debili-
tated him."

Faith stepped forward and looked at the man. A
large red gash lined the side of Christopher's scalp.
He was breathing but not conscious.

"We need to contact the sheriff so he can get
out here to take these men into custody. If they
wake up, they could still harm us," Tabitha stated
with a worried tone.

"How about I go in to town to fetch him,"
Davis volunteered.

"In the meantime, why don't we tie them up?"
Thomas suggested as he reached down and helped
Nathan from the ground. "Where are the other two
men?"

"On the sides of the house," Nathan informed
him.

"Jack and I will go take care of them," Thomas
said, waving for his second son to come with him.
Then gesturing to the captain, he added, "Why
don't you watch him while we do."

"I'll take the girls upstairs and lay them down to
rest," Tabitha said. "This has been quite the ordeal
for them."

Nancy ran forward and wrapped her arms
around Nathan's legs. "I'm so glad you got here

when you did, Nathan. I thought we were going to die for sure."

"Never, Nancy; I'd never let anything happen to you or anyone in the family," Nathan promised, as he patted the young girl's head.

"Come along, Nancy," Tabitha said as she took the girl by the hand and exited the area with her and Ida by her side.

Once everyone left to go about their tasks, Nathan and Faith found themselves alone. Nathan reached out and pulled Faith into his arms. "How are you doing?"

"I'm better now that I know you're unharmed. I was so worried about you."

"God protected all of us like He protected me back in the prison."

"I know He has, and I'm so grateful." Faith glanced towards the captain who was still lying unconscious on the floor. "What an awful man. How can anyone be so vile?"

Nathan's eyes fell to the ground. "Maybe some people are just born to be that way. You heard him; we're just the same."

Faith extended her hand and drew his face up so his eyes met her own. "I hope you heard my response when I told him I know who you are. Let me reassure you, Nathan, you're nothing like that man." Glancing down at the captain, she added, "We should pray for him. No one is a lost cause."

A half hour later, the sheriff, along with several soldiers and a commanding officer from the Confederate Army, showed up at Oak Haven to collect the Union spies.

"Don't trust anything that man says," Nathan warned, handing the Union Captain over to them. "He's trained to lie convincingly. I should know, I taught him how."

The Confederate Colonel nodded. Then glancing between the men, he added, "Since you know him so well, maybe you would consider coming back to do the interrogation. You'd know how to get him to give us what we need better than anyone."

Faith held her breath. Would Nathan agree? She knew he was loyal to the Confederacy, but he still wasn't healed from his captivity. She didn't want him to risk his recovery out of a false sense of obligation.

"I'm sorry, Colonel Mullins, but not only am I in no condition to do that, I have a wedding to attend. I'm rather sure the bride would want me to be there," Nathan explained.

"I do," Faith stated adamantly as she stepped forward and placed her hand on Nathan's arm.

The Colonel gave an understanding smile. "I can't say I blame you. You've given more than your fair share for this war. We'll take these prisoners off your hands and be on our way."

The men left the house, leaving Nathan and Faith alone once more. He turned to Faith, then pulled her towards him. "Your love has saved me, Faith. If I didn't have you, I don't know what would have happened to me."

"And you'll never have to know. I'm yours, forever and always," Faith promised, letting herself melt into his arms, knowing that no matter what came their way, she would be Nathan's for the rest of her life.

EPILOGUE

J ust as Faith promised, Nathan realized the moment he watched his bride walk towards him, she was his forever and always. As Nathan stood under the oak tree outside the church, he knew the same was true for him; his heart, body and soul belonged to Faith Abernathy.

His bride looked breathtaking in her mother's soft white, lace wedding gown, which cascaded down in intricate folds with puffs of tulle at the bottom. Her blonde hair was arranged in curls on top of her head with just a handful of tendrils falling down and around her neck and face.

She was carrying a bouquet of pink and cream flowers in one hand; the other was tucked in the crook of her father's arm as he guided her

JENNA BRANDT

down the path. As she approached him, what stood out the most was Faith's smile. Joy radiated from her and Nathan felt an overwhelming sense of fulfillment. He was right where he was supposed to be.

❦

Faith looked around the courtyard as she walked towards Nathan. Family and friends surrounded them, grinning with excitement as they watched her make her way to the moment when the rest of her life would start.

When she reached Nathan's side, she heard Pastor Howell inquire, "Who gives this woman away?"

Faith's father answered, "I do." Her father kissed her on the cheek and handed her over to Nathan.

One look in her soon-to-be husband's eyes and Faith's stomach somersaulted. She couldn't wait until she was Mrs. Maddox and could spend the rest of her life loving Nathan.

"Friends and family, we're gathered here today to witness the joining of these two people. Nathan and Faith have had a long, and difficult journey to get here, but this day has finally arrived. We have the privilege of being a part of this special day."

Faith stared into her beloved's eyes and squeezed his hands, knowing that what Pastor Howell said was true. They had fought hard to get where they were and to find a way to make a life together, even after the war tried to tear them apart.

As the ceremony continued, Pastor Howell smiled at both of them. "Do you, Faith, take this man to be your husband? To have and to hold from this day forward until your final day?"

"Always and forever," Faith promised.

"And do you, Nathan, take this woman to be your wife? To have and to hold from this day forward until your final day?"

"Always and forever," Nathan echoed.

"Do you have the rings?"

Hope stepped forward from beside Faith and handed a ring to the pastor as did Davis from the other side of Nathan.

"These rings are a symbol of your commitment to each other, a circle never-ending." He handed them the rings and asked them to repeat after him as they placed them on each other's fingers.

"With this ring, I thee wed."

The ring fit perfectly on Faith's finger, and she

cherished it, knowing it would be a constant reminder of the vows she made today.

"By the power vested in me by God, I now pronounce you husband and wife," Pastor Howell announced. With a twinkle in his eye, he added, "Nathan, you may kiss your bride."

Nathan bent down and placed his lips upon Faith's. It was a gentle kiss filled with hope for the future, and forgiveness of the past.

The newlyweds turned to face the townspeople of Myrtle Grove, ready to celebrate with the people they cared most about. As they stood side by side with their fingers intertwined, everyone cheered and clapped.

Faith looked up at her husband and mouthed the words, "I love you."

Nathan mouthed them back, squeezing her hand as they rushed down the walkway and towards the rest of their lives together.

AUTHENTIC CIVIL WAR RECIPE

Molasses Apple Pie

As one can imagine, there were very few treats to be found during the American Civil War. Sugar was scarce, but molasses endured in many kitchens. Added to the fact it was easy to store and transport, the few sweets offered often had the dark liquid substance as a key ingredient. Even with the war raging on, the seasons still changed and what crops that could be harvested were. One of the most consistent crops was apples. A recipe like this would have been easy for anyone short on ingredients, but wanting to satisfy a sweet tooth or celebrate a special occasion.

Ingredients:
- •5 green apples, peeled and sliced
- •1 teaspoon nutmeg
- •1 teaspoon cinnamon
- •1 cup molasses

Line a pie pan with an uncooked pie crust. Fill with sliced apples, nutmeg, cinnamon, and molasses. Cover with a lattice crust and bake at 350 degrees for 1 hour and 15 minutes.

A NOTE FROM THE AUTHOR

I hope you have enjoyed Saved by Faith and plan to continue to read the Civil War Bride series along with my other books. Your opinion and support matters, so I would greatly appreciate you taking the time to leave a review. Without dedicated readers, a storyteller is lost. Thank you for investing in my stories.

Jenna Brandt

Contemporary

Lawfully Adored-K-9

Lawfully Wedded-K-9

Lawfully Treasured-SWAT

Lawfully Dashing-Female Cop/Christmas

Lawfully Devoted-Billionaire Bodyguard/K-9

Lawfully Heroic-Military Police (Coming Soon)

Billionaires of Manhattan Series

The billionaires that live in Manhattan and the women who love them. If you love epic dates, grand romantic gestures, and men in suits with hearts of gold, then these are books are perfect for you.

Waiting on the Billionaire

(Also on Audiobook)

Nanny for the Billionaire

Merging with the Billionaire (coming soon)

Stand-alone Billionaire Book

A billionaire playboy banished to an island, a local girl trying to save her family's legacy. What happens when their worlds collide resulting in a fake marriage?

Billionaire in Disguise

Second Chance with You Series is written by a group of sweet, clean contemporary romance authors connected by the idea that past loves, broken apart for a myriad of reasons, can be brought back together--some by chance, some by circumstance, some by choice.
Jenna's Second Chance book:

Rekindled

Match Made in Heaven Series-standalone stories that are sweet, clean romances designed to whisk you away. Not every man has six-pack abs, nor every woman the model of femininity, but everyone needs someone. We believe in building a world that begins at the very core of what makes romance stories work—faith, hope, and love. Now it's your turn to find love. Set your imagination and heart free with us. The next happily-ever-after is at your fingertips, just waiting to be told…
Jenna's Matched books:

Royally Matched-Contemporary

Discreetly Matched-Historical

Silverpines Series-centered around the fictional town of Silverpines, Oregon, during the turn of the 20th century. When a disaster takes most of the men, the women are left to save the town by placing mail-order groom advertisements. Get to know the various lovable characters and their stories from some of todays bestselling historical authors.

Wanted: Tycoon

Belles of Wyoming Series-centered around the fictional small town of Belle, Wyoming. Each set of books take place during a season of the year.

June's Remedy-Summer

Bride Herder Series-take one failed rancher turned matchmaker and ten unexpected brides at once with no clue as to who wanted them. What could go wrong?

Herd to Please

Mail Order Misfit-a mail order bride story about a woman running from a broken past and a widower with three children who is hiding from a broken heart. What happens when they decide to take a chance on each other?

Mail Order Misfit

The Window to the Heart Saga is a recountal of the epic journey of Lady Margaret, a young English noblewoman, who through many trials, obstacles, and tragedies, discovers her own inner strength, the sustaining force of faith in God, and the power of family and friends. In this three-part series, experience new places and cultures as the heroine travels from England to France and completes her adventures in America. The series has compelling themes of love, loss, faith and hope with an exceptionally gratifying conclusion.

Trilogy

The English Proposal (Book 1)

The French Encounter (Book 2)

The American Conquest (Book 3)

Spin-offs

The Oregon Pursuit (Book 1)

The White Wedding (Book 2)

The Christmas Bride (Book 3)

The Viscount's Wife (Book 4)

The Window to the Heart Saga

Trilogy Box Set

The Window to the Heart Saga

Spin-off Books Box Set

The Window to the Heart Saga

Complete Collection Box Set

For more information about Jenna Brandt visit her on any of her websites.

www.JennaBrandt.com

Jenna Brandt's Reader Group

www.facebook.com/JennaBrandtAuthor

www.twitter.com/JennaDBrandt

Signup for Jenna Brandt's Newsletter

JOIN MY MAILING LIST AND READER'S GROUP

<u>Sign-up for my newsletter and get a FREE story.</u>

<u>Join my Reader Group and get access to exclusive content and contests.</u>

ACKNOWLEDGMENTS

My writing journey would not be possible without those who supported me. Since I can remember, writing is the only thing I love to do, and my deepest desire is to share my talent with others.

First and foremost, I am eternally grateful to Jesus, my lord and savior, who created me with this "writing bug" DNA.

In addition, many thanks go to:

My husband, Dustin, and three daughters, Katie, Julie, and Nikki, for loving me and supporting me during all my late-night writing marathons and coffee-infused mornings.

My mother, Connie, for being my first and most honest critic, now and always. As a little girl, sleeping under your desk during late-night deadlines for the local paper showed me what being a dedicated writer looked like.

My angels in heaven: my grandmother, who passed away in 2001; my infant son, Dylan, who was taken by SIDS five years ago; and my father, who left us three years ago.

To my ARC Angels for taking the time to read my story and give valuable feedback.

And lastly, but so important, to my dedicated readers, who have shared their love of my books with others, helping to spread the words about my stories. Your devotion means a great deal.

ABOUT THE AUTHOR

Jenna Brandt is an award-winning, international best selling, historical and contemporary romance author. Her historical books span from the Victorian to Western eras and all of her books have elements of romance, suspense and faith. Her debut series, the Window to the Heart Saga, as well as her Billionaires of Manhattan Series, have become bestselling series, and her multi-author series, The Lawkeepers, Silverpines, Belles of Wyoming, and Bride Herders are fan-favorites.

She has been an avid reader since she could hold a book and started writing stories almost as early. She has been published in several newspapers as well as edited for multiple papers. She graduated with her Bachelor of Arts in English from Bethany College and was the Editor-in-Chief of the newspaper while there. Her first blog was published on Yahoo Parenting and The Grief Toolbox as well as featured on the ABC News and Good Morning America websites.

Writing is her passion, but she also enjoys cooking, watching movies, reading, engaging in social media and spending time with her three young daughters and husband where they live in the Central Valley of California. She is also active in her local church where she volunteers on their first impressions team.

Made in the USA
Monee, IL
09 April 2022